CHAINED FATE

MOLOTOV BETROTHAL: BOOK 3

ANNA ZAIRES

♠ MOZAIKA PUBLICATIONS ♠

Copyright © 2025 Anna Zaires and Dima Zales
www.annazaires.com

Published by Mozaika Publications, an imprint of Mozaika LLC.
www.mozaikallc.com

Cover by Alex McLaughlin

Photography by Regina Wamba
www.reginawamba.com

ISBN: 979-8-89796-023-1

CHAPTER 1

ALINA

The pilot's announcement that our plane is starting its descent into Geneva cuts through the heavy fog of sleep engulfing me. I try to open my eyes, but they feel swollen and gritty, my lids all but glued shut. I must've fallen asleep again while crying in Alexei's embrace. I give up and keep my eyes closed. My head is throbbing anew, and my nausea is returning. I don't know if the latter is from my early pregnancy or the tumor eating my brain, and I don't particularly care. It's also possible my stomach is revolting from the knowledge of what awaits me when we land.

Awake brain surgery.

Chemo.

Radiation.

Loss of our baby.

For some reason, the last one is the hardest to come to terms with. If I proceed with the surgery and the treatment, the tiny embryo inside me—which I'm convinced is a girl—won't survive. But if I don't, *I* won't survive, and Alexei won't allow that.

I want to cry all over again.

I'm also pathetically, embarrassingly grateful that he seems determined to see this through with me. I don't know how long his resolve will last once he sees me truly sick, but a part of me wants to believe him, to trust him. Not that I have a choice. He refuses to let me go home to my brothers… and some perverse part of me is grateful for that too.

A warm, heavy hand lands on my bare arm and strokes it softly. I swallow the burning knot in my throat and force open my eyes to meet my new husband's intense, dark gaze.

Alexei's face is still drawn tight, still tired. I wonder if he's gotten any sleep since we left the yacht. Somehow, I doubt it.

The urge to touch him, to soothe him, wells up again. It's insidious, the way the cruel, sardonic curve of his mouth now seems to hold a promise of tenderness, how his hard, mercilessly sculpted features are becoming so achingly familiar to me. Despite everything, my skin tingles at his touch, my heartbeat picking up pace at his proximity, and I know that if he were to lean down and press his lips to mine, the scorching heat of our connection would burn away all reason, all reality.

But he won't do that. Because we're landing soon and going straight to the clinic, where the doctors will cut open my skull and excise as much of the tumor as they can.

The thought is like a wet rag slapped against my face.

I swallow against another surge of nausea and sit up. "Where are my clothes?"

I was in a dress before embarking on our submarine journey that somehow ended with us on this private jet, but right now, I'm wearing only his black T-shirt that's hugely oversized on me.

"I undressed you so you'd be more comfortable sleeping," Alexei says, standing up. He walks over to a small door I didn't notice before and opens it, revealing a tiny closet that holds only the dress and the underwear I was wearing. His expression is apologetic as he turns to me. "I didn't think to grab any clean clothes for either of us. Sorry about that."

"It's okay." I'm guessing he had his hands full, figuring out how to get us here from the other side of the planet and all—though I do wish I had my makeup at the very least. I can feel how puffy my eyes are, and I'm sure I look terrible.

And the worst hasn't even started.

Ugh. I wish I could turn off that voice in my head, the one that sounds suspiciously like my mom's. Who cares what I look like when I'm fucking *dying*? I need to focus on what truly matters, not something as shallow as whether I'll lose my hair all at once or in patches.

Alexei returns to the bed, carrying my underwear and the dress. Wordlessly, he hands them to me, and I flush, realizing he expects me to change right here, in front of him. It's not an illogical expectation, given that he's my husband whose seed is still crusted on my thighs. But my face burns regardless as I snatch the clothes from him and jump off the bed, ignoring the wave of nausea accompanying the sudden motion.

"I'll be right back," I mutter as I beeline for the bathroom.

I need a shower at the very least.

"You don't have much time," Alexei calls after me. "We're landing in seventeen minutes."

"Got it!" Swiftly, I strip off his shirt and hop in the small shower stall. There's no time to wash and blow-dry my hair, so I put it up in a lopsided ballerina bun and focus on rinsing off all traces of our sexfest.

When I'm done, I dry myself, dress in the clothes I was wearing, and pull my hair into a more artful messy bun. As expected, my face is a disaster, all pale, blotchy skin and puffy eyes, but I doubt the doctors will care. And if Alexei doesn't like what he sees... oh, well. The sooner he realizes he's made a mistake sticking by me, the better.

Alexei is waiting impatiently when I emerge. "We need to take our seats. Let's go."

Before I can reply, he shepherds me into the main cabin of the plane. It's spacious and luxurious, which doesn't surprise me in the least. Like my family, the Leonovs are obscenely rich and have never shied away from using their wealth.

Ruslan, Alexei's younger brother, looks up from his

laptop when we take our seats next to him. His storm-gray eyes are uncharacteristically gentle as he meets my gaze. "Hey," he says softly. "How are you doing?"

A couple of days ago, I would've snapped back with something sarcastic along the lines of, "How do you think?" But I don't have the energy for belligerence, and there's something so genuine in the concern on his hard features that my chest pinches with unwelcome emotion.

"I'm okay," I mumble and focus on buckling myself in so I don't do something embarrassing, like start crying again. I know Ruslan doesn't truly care about me—he probably hates me, in fact—but he does care about his brother and what my diagnosis means for him... and illogically, so do I.

Alexei shouldn't have manipulated our families into betrothing us when I was fifteen. He shouldn't have stalked me for a decade or stormed my brother's Idaho compound to force me into marriage. And he certainly shouldn't have impregnated me against my will. But he *has* done all those things, and it was because he wanted me. Some fantasy version of me, I'm still convinced of that, but regardless, as much as I resent him for everything he's done, I also can't help but empathize.

It must be terrible to want something so badly and then to finally acquire it, only to have it snatched away from you by a cruel whim of fate... almost as terrible as not wanting something, having it forced upon you, and belatedly realizing you'd do anything to keep it.

My hand unconsciously covers my stomach, and I

look up to find Ruslan staring at it. Flushing again, I move my hand away and fix my gaze on the circular window. I'm sure Alexei's brother is fully informed of the situation, but I still don't feel right broadcasting my barely-there pregnancy, especially given where it's heading.

Outside, the thick cloud cover is receding to reveal the postcard-pretty Lake Geneva and the peaks of the snowy Alps. Normally, I'd enjoy the view, but now, I just close my eyes and listen to the changing hum of the engines as our descent steepens.

A big male hand covers mine on the armrest, and I know without looking that it's Alexei lending me his warmth and strength. The sucky part is, I need it. His touch chases away some of the cold dread suffocating me, and a part of me wishes we were back on the yacht, just us and the endless ocean, back in the good old days when he was my biggest enemy, my worst fear.

I keep my eyes closed as I hear the screeching rumble of the wheels emerging from the belly of the jet and feel a soft jolt as said wheels make contact with the runway.

This is it.

We have arrived.

Within minutes, we disembark at a small private airport, where a luxury electric SUV is waiting for us. Alexei helps me into the back seat while Ruslan goes to sit up front with the driver, and then we're on our way, the car's smooth, soundless ride perversely aggravating.

I want jolts and bumps, the roar of a motor, anything to distract me from where we're going and what's going to happen there.

As if reading my mind, Alexei lays a hand on my thigh. "It's going to be okay." His voice is low and steady. "They won't hurt you, I promise. I'll be with you every step of the way." His dark gaze is unwavering as his eyes catch mine.

A tiny bit of tension drains out of me. I don't know why that promise makes a difference, but it does. I still don't want to be his wife, still resent him for binding us together against my will, but there's something perversely reassuring in knowing that he still wants me, that he's not afraid to face this horror with me.

He keeps his hand on my leg for the rest of the ride, and I don't pull away. To distract myself from what's coming, I keep my gaze trained on his hand, studying the imperfect ovals of his short, bluntly filed nails, the small scars on the edges of his callused fingers, the veins underneath his darkly tanned skin. It's a strong, rough hand, one capable of terrifying brutality... and even more terrifying tenderness.

Finally, we're there, parking in front of a pretty four-story building that looks like it was built a few centuries ago. I blink and finally look around. I've been to Geneva more than once, and though I don't know exactly where we are, the cobblestone streets and the presence of tourists tells me we're not far from the popular Old Town area.

It's not where I would've expected a cutting-edge

medical facility to be located, but what do I know? It's a nice area, that's for sure.

Alexei helps me out of the car as though I were already disabled, but I don't mind. Nor do I mind his hand on my lower back, its weight and warmth gently supportive. My knees feel weak and shaky, and my heart beats much too fast as we enter the building—which looks much more modern on the inside, with the reception area decorated in soothing blue-gray hues. Live plants in clay pots line the reception counter, adding a touch of life and warmth to the cool interior, as does a lush, six-foot-tall potted cane to the right of the reception desk.

Before we can approach the receptionist, a pretty blonde who looks to be in her late teens, the doors behind her swing open, and two middle-aged men in white coats emerge. I swallow hard as they approach us with broad, welcoming smiles.

"Mr. and Mrs. Leonov," the shorter one says in lightly accented British English. "It is such a pleasure to meet you both. I'm Dr. Ingels, and this is my colleague, Dr. Fasseau. We work with Dr. Kressler. Dr. Fasseau will perform the operation, and I will assist him with it."

Alexei nods, his jaw tight. "Let's get on with it."

The doctors look taken aback. Like most Western Europeans, they're used to at least a modicum of polite chitchat. Alexei is clearly not in the mood to indulge them, and neither am I. They regroup quickly, however.

"Please, follow us," Fasseau says. "We'll start by running a few more tests, beginning with a more thorough MRI."

Great. Another hour with all the clanking and beeping noises—just what my throbbing head needs. But it would be foolish to object. Since they're going to be cutting into my brain, I want them to be *very* sure about what they're doing. And there's a tiny part of me that's still hoping that maybe, just maybe, I was misdiagnosed. That the supposed tumor was the result of a faulty MRI machine on the submarine—it was a portable one, after all.

Alexei doesn't say anything either. Silently, we follow the two doctors down a hallway and to a small, cozy room, one wall of which is occupied by two large lockers.

"You can change here," Ingels says. "You can find a dressing gown and slippers in either of the lockers. Please be sure to remove all jewelry and anything that may contain metal. You don't have a pacemaker or any implanted devices, correct?"

"Correct," I say.

"Good," Fasseau says. "We'll have you fill out a more detailed form before the test begins, but for now, please go ahead and change. Oh, and if you need to use the bathroom, now would be a good time, as the scan will take at least an hour and a half."

I wince, my headache worsening at the mere thought of it. But there's nothing to be done, so I just wait for the doctors to depart, which they do promptly.

Alexei stays, however, his expression dark and concerned as he steps up to me.

"Are you okay?" he asks softly, laying his hand on my upper arm. "If you want to rest for a few minutes before—"

I shake my head. "No. I'm fine. Well… not fine, but you know."

"Yeah." His face tightens, even as he gently rubs his palm up and down my arm. "I know."

I stare up at him, the peculiar impulse to touch him returning. I want to kiss the hard, grim line of his lips and smooth the new lines of tension bracketing his mouth, to trace my knuckles over the uncompromising line of his jaw and run my fingertips over the rough, dark stubble on his cheeks.

Though by all rights, he's still my adversary, it no longer feels like it. It feels like we're a team, like we're in this together… because even though I'm the one who's sick, he's suffering too.

I can see it, and it hurts me—and I don't understand why.

The rhythm of his breathing alters, his dark eyes heating up. As always, he can sense the fatal weakness within me, the way I'm drawn to him against my will. And this time, it's not purely physical, this urge that's growing within me. It's something deeper, more reso-nant… more dangerous.

I should run from it. I should fight it with all my might. But I can't—if only because I'm saving all the fight in me for the upcoming battle for my life. Or at least that's the excuse I'll tell myself later, when I'm beating myself up for what I'm about to do.

For *this*.

I grip his face between my palms, rise up onto my tiptoes, and press my lips to his.

CHAPTER 2

ALEXEI

For the first few moments, I'm convinced that I've fallen asleep on the plane and am now caught in a nightmare that's taken a sudden turn into a wet dream. What else can explain the fact that Alina's soft lips are pressed to mine, her tongue venturing boldly into my mouth while her delicate hands cradle my face, even as the two doctors stand right outside the thin wall of this changing room, waiting to perform an MRI that will confirm her deadly diagnosis?

But no. No dream has ever felt this real. Not to mention, my head still feels like it's been run over by a tank, the lack of sleep a leaden weight on every cell in my body.

No, scratch that. Not every cell. A bunch of cells are definitely alert and defying gravity. And as more blood rushes in that direction, igniting the violent fire that always burns in me for this woman, I forget all about said lack of sleep and our unfortunate location.

Because my Alinyonok is kissing me.

Kissing and touching me of her own accord.

A low growl rumbles in my chest, and I kiss her back, fiercely, savagely, gripping her hips hard. I try to be gentle, I really fucking do, but she makes it impossible. Instead of being passive and pliant in my embrace, she tears at my clothes, pushing at me with all the strength in her slender frame. I let her push me where she wants, and my back hits the metal doors of the lockers with a clang. The loud sound should've brought us to our senses, but nothing can penetrate the bubble of heat and madness encasing us—and certainly not once she unzips my pants and slips her hand inside, curling it around my throbbing dick while her mouth is still glued to mine.

That's the point at which I lose it. Or maybe I passed that point long ago. Perhaps when I first saw her. All I know is that as her slender fingers squeeze my shaft and begin to stroke up and down, my balls draw up tight and my vision blurs, my labored breaths roaring in my ears. My hands act of their own accord, lifting her up against me and shoving aside her underwear as she wraps her long legs around my hips. And then… fuuuck. Oh, fuck. My nerve endings buzz with electrifying tension as my cock sinks into her wet, hot, silky flesh, sliding in so deep that she cries out, momentarily breaking our kiss.

I groan too, trying to slow down, to hold on to any

semblance of control, but as always, it is futile. She's back to kissing me—devouring me, in fact—and I am burning up, overtaken by the dark heat of it, the sheer fucking madness. I don't know what this is, why she's suddenly initiating sex when she's always claimed not to want me, but I don't fucking care. *This* is how I've always known it could be between us; this feral hunger is what I've always sensed in her.

She's as desperate for me as I am for her, and for once, she's not fighting it. She's not fighting *me*. Instead, the current battle is between our bodies. Her tight, wet flesh clamps down on my cock as she rides me with all she's got, milking me, trying to make me explode, whereas I'm trying to prolong this, to draw out the ecstasy prickling my spine, to make *her* explode first. And then… fuck! I throw my head back as I lose—and win.

We come together, my guttural groan blending with her cry as we reach the peak and go over it, the pleasure crashing over us with a violence that leaves us both drained and shaking, our harsh breaths audible in the small room.

I don't know what I expect in the aftermath. Or maybe I do. Because with Alina, it's always one step forward, two steps back. Not to mention she's likely embarrassed that we were almost certainly overheard. But she surprises me. As our bodies separate, instead of pulling away and acting like I've just done something monstrous to her, Alina lays her head on my shoulder and wraps her arms around my waist, leaning against me, letting me embrace her for another minute.

Letting us both pretend that this is the start of something new and wonderful, that everything is going to be all right.

And it will be. I'm determined to make it so. To that end... I gently pull away and lift her chin with the crook of my fingers, forcing her to meet my gaze. "Ready for the scan?"

She nods, biting her puffy-from-our-kisses lips. But then she grimaces wryly and looks down at herself. "Actually... I think I could use a quick trip to the restroom first."

Because my cum is dripping down her legs. Of course. I could use some cleanup too. I glance down at my cock, still wet from being inside her, and then I tuck it back into my pants and zip up.

I need to order us both a change of clothes, pronto.

The two doctors avert their gazes as we emerge from the dressing room. "Where is the bathroom?" I ask coolly.

Fasseau clears his throat. "There's one by the reception area and one back there. I can take your wife to one, and Dr. Ingels will escort you to the other."

Alina is already hurrying past me to the indicated bathroom by the reception, her face pink as she avoids looking at either of the doctors. Fasseau goes after her, and I let Ingels show me where the other bathroom is.

Maybe it's all the endorphins from our impromptu encounter in the dressing room, or maybe it's the fact that she initiated said encounter, but I feel better. I feel… optimistic. No, that's not it. I feel *certain* that everything will work out—that Alina will get well, and that she'll grow to love me, as I've always known she would.

We just have to get through this surgery and whatever comes afterward.

Once inside the small, impeccably modern bathroom, I clean up the best I can and splash cold water on my face to fight off another wave of tiredness. I'm not going to rest until after Alina's surgery is done. If she's going to be awake while her skull is cut open, then fuck knows, so will I.

I will hold her hand through it all, and I will be by her bedside when she wakes for good.

Exiting, I tell Ingels to bring me to Alina. I assume, being a woman, she needs a little longer to clean up than I do.

He leads me to the bathroom by the entrance, and then we wait. And wait. And fucking wait.

After a couple more minutes, I turn to Ingels. "Where's your colleague? Did he already take her in for the scan?"

Ingels frowns. "Maybe." He steps up to the bathroom door and knocks on it lightly. "Mrs. Leonov? Are you in there?"

No answer.

"I guess he must've taken her there already," Ingels says, looking a bit puzzled. "Let's go."

I follow him down the hallway again, a peculiar

unease stirring in my chest. We find Fasseau in the MRI room, talking to two techs.

It doesn't look like the machine is running—and Alina is nowhere to be seen.

"Where's my wife?" I ask sharply.

Fasseau turns to face me. "Oh, Mr. Leonov, hello. I was just wondering that myself. I asked Miss Weiss, our receptionist, to escort her here when she's done. Is she not in the—"

I'm already running. No, I'm *sprinting* for the bathroom by the reception. It takes me only seconds to cover the distance at this speed, and then I'm pounding on the bathroom door and rattling the doorknob—which won't fucking give.

"Mr. Leonov! Please, Mr. Leonov, let us get the key!"

The shouts of the doctors reach me just as I step back and slam my foot into the bathroom door, causing it to creak and crack. I kick it again, ignoring the shock of pain radiating up my leg, and the door flies open, squeaking as it hangs partially off the hinges. The doctors gasp at the destruction, as does the young receptionist who's hurried over to watch the spectacle, but I don't give a fuck.

Contrary to my worst fears, there's no Alina lying passed out inside.

There's nothing but a small open window looking out onto the tourist-filled street.

CHAPTER 3

ALINA

My heart drums in a dizzying beat as I walk fast, passing two tour groups. I still can't believe I'm out here, on the streets of Geneva... that I escaped.

I didn't plan on it.

I didn't even think it was possible.

When I entered the small bathroom to clean up, escape was the last thing on my mind. But there was that small open window, and suddenly, it dawned on me that I was in Geneva. Not in the middle of the Pacific, stuck on a yacht with no way out. Not in some heavily armed compound in Russia, where Alexei will likely have me reside.

No, I was in a regular medical facility in the middle of Old Town Geneva, and this was my chance.

I didn't think twice about it. I didn't analyze the consequences and implications. I just climbed up on the windowsill, wriggled my head and shoulders through the opening, and tumbled out, hands first, onto the cobblestone street.

Now my palms are scraped, and one wrist may or may not be sprained, but I have escaped.

I am free.

I turn the corner, heading for the lakefront. I don't know where I'm going, but my instinct is to stay with the crowds, to blend in as much as possible. A clothing store appears to my right, and I hurry in there, only to remember that I don't have my wallet or phone or anything that would allow me to pay—or to contact my brothers.

That is… assuming I *want* to contact my brothers.

I stop in front of a stylishly dressed mannequin, suddenly nauseated as the headache returns, squeezing my temples in a brutal vise. The initial euphoria of my impromptu escape is wearing off, and I'm realizing that I'm not out of the woods. Far from it.

For one thing, I'm less than five blocks from the clinic, and Alexei could find me at any moment. But even if I were to miraculously evade him and return to my family, what am I going to do if Alexei goes back on his word and comes after Nikolai and Slava again? Technically, I upheld our bargain by marrying him, but what if that's not how he sees it? Not to mention, he could come after my other brothers in an effort to get me back. Assuming he'd want me back, given the diagnosis.

And that's another thing. The diagnosis. Running away doesn't change the fact that a tumor is growing in my brain—and a baby in my stomach. Those two are still as incompatible as ever, and the thought of having to make those agonizing choices without Alexei, of facing any of it without him… I swallow, my throat burning, and turn away from the mannequin before the saleswoman behind the counter notices the tears that are suddenly veiling my vision.

Dammit. How pathetic am I? I shouldn't need Alexei for moral support, or for anything, really. I have no idea what came over me today, why I attacked him in the dressing room like a sex-starved felon, but I'm going to chalk that up to momentary stress-induced madness. Or maybe early-pregnancy hormones. That's a thing, right? Either way, I refuse to need a man who manipulated, threatened, and murdered his way into my life.

Whatever anxiety I'm feeling at the thought of being away from him is, more than likely, some manifestation of Stockholm syndrome or whatever abused wives feel for their controlling husbands. Not that he's ever been abusive toward me, but I can't forget what kind of man he is… or how marriage to that kind of man turned out for my mother.

Fuck. Now I'm *really* nauseated.

I hurry out of the store and run into a small alley, where I fall onto all fours and retch next to a dumpster, my head throbbing with a violence that makes me want to curl up and die.

"Too much to drink?" asks a German-accented

female voice, and I somehow find the strength to lift my head.

I find a tall, lean blonde with a dozen facial piercings regarding me with a sympathetic smile from a few steps away. Before I can respond, she walks over and crouches next to me, handing me a packet of wet wipes and a stainless-steel bottle. "Here. This should help."

If I weren't so miserable, I would never impose on a stranger like this, but I am and I accept the offering. Staying on my knees, I pull out two wipes and clean my face and hands before opening the bottle to take a sip of what turns out to be lemon-flavored water. I swish it around before spitting it out. Then I take another sip that I swallow. Thankfully, it stays down, even though the nausea is still intense.

"Thank you." I throw the used wipes in the dumpster and hand the bottle and the unused wipes back to her. My voice is rough and scratchy, barely recognizable as mine as I say, "That's very kind of you."

She shrugs and grins. "Hey, we've all been there, right?"

I manage a weak smile back. I doubt many people have been in my exact situation, but I'm not going to get into that with her. She looks to be about my age, and judging by the well-worn backpack slung over her shoulders, she's likely traveling around Europe, enjoying being young and carefree.

"Thanks again," I say and force myself to rise to my feet. A wave of dizziness nearly fells me, and she notices, grabbing my arm to hold me upright before I can grab on to the edge of the trash receptacle to steady myself.

"Hey there, you okay?" Her pierced brows furrow as she studies me. "Do you need me to get any medical help?"

"No, I'm—" I take a deep breath to quell another surge of nausea. "I'm okay, thanks."

"Uh-huh." She doesn't look convinced. "You don't smell like alcohol."

"Yeah, no, I…" I hesitate, then decide to give her a portion of the truth. "I'm pregnant."

Her sky-blue eyes widen. "Oh. Gotcha." She scans me up and down, her eyes lingering on my flat stomach. "Still pretty early, huh?"

I grimace. "Very."

She must realize that she's still propping me up because she asks, "Are you able to stand?" At my nod, she lets go of me, steps back, and scans me again. Her gaze narrows. "Do you have a phone or anything?"

"Umm, no. I… forgot my purse."

"Do you need me to call anyone for you? Take you anywhere? Do you live here, or are you visiting?" She throws out the questions without pausing for a single breath. Before I can begin to reply, she says, "Never mind. Let's get you away from this stinky trash first. My hostel is right next door."

Gripping my arm again, she tows me to a weather-beaten door in the alley that I hadn't noticed before. Bemused, I let myself get dragged into what turns out to be a small, dimly lit lounge populated by several gently worn recliners and tables. An unmanned reception desk is on the other end. A rickety-looking spiral staircase occupies one of the corners, and two young women descend it, laughing and chatting in Italian before exiting out of a set of doors on the opposite wall.

A hostel. How interesting. I've never been in one. Come to think of it, I've never been in a hotel that wasn't five stars or better.

The blonde drags me to one of the recliners and pushes me into it. "Sit. I'll be right back."

She disappears up the staircase and reappears a minute later with a tall glass of water and a packet of candies. Ginger candies, I note with surprise as she hands them to me.

"I get motion-sick, and these help," she explains. "Supposed to be good for pregnancy too."

"Thanks. That's so nice of you." I gladly chug the water and stick a candy in my mouth. It's sweet and spicy, and I'm not sure how much it's helping, but I'm too grateful to the blonde to spit it out. Instead, I transfer it to one cheek and say, "I'm Alina. And you are?"

"Birgit." She cocks her head, studying me. "You're not American, are you? The way you said your name..."

"Oh, yeah, I'm from Russia. I studied at an American school, though, so..."

"Ah, that explains the accent. Or lack of it." She plops into the chair opposite me. "I was hoping to visit Russia this year, but I got talked out of it. Unsafe for a young Western woman traveling alone and all that."

"It probably is," I admit. And not just for a young Western woman. My brothers never let me go anywhere without a bodyguard—though that was mostly due to all the enemies my family had acquired in their ruthless climb to the top.

Enemies that include the Leonovs, my husband's family.

At the thought of Alexei, a peculiar heaviness settles low in my stomach. It's not anxiety or fear, but something more ill-defined, an unease that feels almost like... guilt.

No, that's ridiculous. I can't possibly feel guilty that I ran. I don't owe Alexei anything, no matter what happened between us during that momentary madness. My husband—or more appropriately, my *stalker*—took away my freedom. He took away all my choices. So when I saw an opportunity for escape, I went for it. It's what anyone would do in my situation... right?

"—or living here?"

I blink, realizing I tuned Birgit out. "Sorry, say that again?"

Thankfully, she doesn't seem offended by my lack of attention. "Are you visiting or living here?" she asks, carefully enunciating each word.

Maybe she thinks pregnancy is messing with my brain. Which is possible. Along with the other thing. Which is more than possible, given that it's a *fucking tumor in my brain.*

Shit. I'm spacing again. "Just visiting," I say before she writes me off as a total ditz. "What about you? Why are you here?"

She makes a face. "I'm… finding myself, I guess. I did all the right things—went to a university, got a degree, got a boring-ass office job in Frankfurt, got an apartment, and then… then my mom got sick. Breast cancer. She died six months ago, and I realized life is too fucking short not to do what you want. You know? So I'm trying to figure out what that is. I know it's not my boring-ass job or the boring-ass life I had before."

I bite my lip. "I'm sorry about your mom."

She nods, blinking too rapidly. "Yeah, thanks. It's no longer as raw, but it still fucking sucks. She was only fifty-two. Way too young for that shit, you know?"

I do know. God, I wish I didn't. But this is not about me. I reach out and cover Birgit's hand with mine, squeezing gently. "It does fucking suck."

She stares at our hands, then looks up with an overly bright smile. "So yeah, that's my story. What's yours?"

Hmm, let's see. I was betrothed to the son of my family's enemies at fifteen and did my best to evade him for a decade while he stalked me and killed every boy and man who expressed any interest in me. Said evasion ended when he stormed my brother's compound with a small army, abducting me and forcing me to marry him. Oh, and I've just learned I'm pregnant with his child and have brain cancer.

Yeah, I'm not telling her any of this. "Just visiting Geneva to see the sights, et cetera."

She nods sagely. "Getting in all the travel before the baby comes, huh?"

"Something like that."

Her gaze drops to my left hand, where Alexei's ring is still adorning my finger. "You're married?"

"Hmm-mm." I transfer the ginger candy to my other cheek.

She cocks her head. "Where is your husband?"

Probably out looking for me. And before long, he'll find me, bringing my impromptu escape attempt to an end.

I take a deep breath. This is it. This is my chance to ask Birgit for her phone so I can call my brothers and get the ball rolling on an actual escape. Except… I would be endangering them. I mean, I know my brothers can more than take care of themselves and have the resources to fight off whatever my husband throws at them, but still, Alexei is ruthless, and he's demonstrated that he's willing to go to insane lengths to get me. Or *was* willing. Either way, I can't risk more bloodshed on my behalf.

"He's…" I pause because I honestly don't know what to tell her. "We're temporarily separated," I finally improvise.

"Ah." She gives my stomach a sympathetic look. "I see."

"It's… complicated."

"Uh-huh." She meets my gaze. "I just got out of a 'complicated' relationship myself. The asshole cheated on me while my mom was in hospice. So if you want to talk or anything…"

"Thank you, but I should get going." I get up—and nearly puke again as a wave of nauseating dizziness crashes into me.

Gasping, I sink back down and bend in half, tucking my head between my knees while sucking on the candy to stave off the black spots dotting my vision.

"Shit. Are you okay?" Birgit crouches next to me. "Are you sure you don't want to go to a clinic or anything?"

"No, I'm…" I manage to lift my head. "I'm okay. Just nauseated again, that's all."

"You poor thing." She pats my arm as I put my head back down again. "This right here is one of the many reasons I got my tubes tied at twenty-one. Pregnancy sucks, birth is a nightmare, and then you're stuck with a selfish little demon who consumes scarce resources and adds to global warming. No shade on those who decide to procreate, of course," she adds belatedly.

I laugh. I can't help it. I laugh until tears run down my face, and I realize I'm actually crying. Because I want a selfish little demon. I want the pregnancy with all its aches and pains, and the nightmare of a birth, and the exhaustion of postpartum. I want to experience it all, and odds are that I won't. Not with this baby, not with any other.

Even if I were to forego surgery and all the rest, I may not survive long enough to give birth. Not if the cancer is aggressive enough.

It's damned if I do, fucked if I don't.

"Oh, no. Don't cry. I'm so, so sorry." Birgit sounds like she's going to cry herself as she pats my shaking shoulders. "I really didn't mean to upset you. I didn't mean—"

"It's okay." I sit up and rub at my wet face. "Seriously, it's not your fault. I'm just a hormonal, emotional mess right now."

"Right, right." She sits back on her haunches, visibly relieved. "Do you want to come upstairs and rest for a bit? I share a room with two other girls, but they're gone for the day, so it's nice and private right now. You can crash in my bed and—"

"That is so kind of you, thank you. But I can't." I force myself to stand up and not sway despite another wave of dizziness. "I really do have to go."

The longer I stay here, the more likely Alexei is to find me. If he's looking, of course. But I'm going to assume that he is and act accordingly, which means leaving before he catches up to me.

"Go where?" Birgit asks, frowning as she rises to her feet as well. "You can barely stand. Unless… do you want me to call someone for you? Can anyone come get you? A friend? Some family, maybe?"

I shake my head, sucking on the candy for all I'm worth.

I honestly don't know what I'm doing. The full implications of my predicament are just beginning to dawn on me. I can't contact any of my friends or family without putting them in Alexei's crosshairs, and without their help, I might as well return to Alexei right now. Even if he didn't have unlimited resources with which to find me, I literally have nowhere to go. I have no money—or rather, I have lots of money but no obvious way to access it—and no documents. I can't book a hotel, or take a cab, or cross the border. Or buy food, for that matter.

My stomach chooses that very moment to growl, as if to emphasize the seriousness of that last problem.

Birgit's frown deepens. "Are you in some kind of trouble?" Her eyes widen, as if with sudden comprehension, and she lowers her voice. "Is it your husband?"

I try not to react. But I must flinch or otherwise give myself away because her expression turns grim and she nods, as if I've confirmed something.

"It's not what you think," I say quickly, but I can see it's too late.

She thinks Alexei is a danger to me, which he's not. Only to those around me.

For now, a tiny voice reminds me. *Don't forget your father.*

I shut out that voice and focus on convincing Birgit. "It's really not like that."

"Then why are you out here all alone, with no phone or anything?" she asks, clearly not believing me.

She runs her gaze over me. "You're dressed like a million bucks, but you look like you're on death's door."

There is a question in that statement, one I could ignore if I wanted. My predicament is none of her business. But she's been so genuinely nice to me that I don't want to ice her out. Or to lie to her any more than I have to.

"That's... accurate," I say, deciding to go for a portion of the truth. I swallow the gingery juices that have pooled in my mouth, hoping to quell the worsening nausea. "I just got a not-so-good diagnosis. My husband is pushing for immediate treatment, but I'm not sure if I want that, given the pregnancy. So I just... walked away from him for a bit."

"Oh." Her eyes widen. "Oh, shit. I'm sorry."

"It's okay." I force a smile. "That's life for you, right? Anyway, thank you again for everything. I hope you find what you're looking for in your travels."

My legs are not fully steady as I head to the door that the two young women disappeared through. I assume it leads to the street, and I'm right. I'm about to step outside when Birgit's hand lands on my shoulder.

"Look," she says when I turn around. "I don't know the specifics of your situation, but it sounds like you need some time and space to process things. At least that's what my mom wanted when she first got diagnosed. My dad was pushing for one thing, her siblings for another, and she just wanted a chance to come to terms with it on her own. So yeah..." She takes a deep breath. "If you want that too, you can chill here for a couple of days. Get your head straight before you decide anything."

"Thank you, but I couldn't possibly—"

"You won't be imposing," she says, anticipating my objection. "I could use the company—but only if you want to stay, of course. I promise I won't pry or push you into any decisions you're not ready to make."

She waits, staring at me expectantly, and I honestly don't know what to say. Despite what she's saying, it would be an imposition. A huge one. If I understand correctly, she only has one bed in this place, and we'd have to share it. And I wouldn't even be able to pay her for it. Also, Alexei is bound to find me if I don't stay on the move. Unless… he would be expecting me to stay on the move.

In fact, he'd probably expect me to get out of Geneva as fast as possible.

But no. I can't. She has no idea what kind of man I'm running from. I don't think I would be placing *her* in danger—Alexei would have no reason to come in here with guns blazing—but still, what if—

A sudden worsening of my headache scrambles my thoughts. It's like someone has decided to put my skull in a nutcracker and *squeeze* until my eyeballs pop.

Gasping, I sink to the floor, so nauseated by the throbbing pain that I can barely breathe, black dots flickering with white behind my closed eyelids.

"Right," Birgit says. "Come on now. Let's get you into bed."

I groan as she pulls me to my feet. "I... won't be great company," I manage to say, and she laughs quietly.

"Yeah, I'm getting that vibe. Let's go anyway."

Looping an arm around my waist, she guides me to the stairs.

CHAPTER 4

ALEXEI

"What the fuck do you mean she hasn't been spotted?" I bark at Chekhov, our head of security.

Judiciously, he backs away. This whole clusterfuck is his fault, and he knows it. He was supposed to have guards at the clinic by the time we arrived, but their plane departed Moscow late due to bad weather, and we beat them to the clinic by about an hour. I figured it was no big deal, as the Molotovs were unlikely to triangulate our location that quickly, and I didn't want to delay Alina's surgery by so much as a minute. Stupidly, I didn't think she would run. Not after fucking me like that.

Not when her freaking *life* is on the line.

Motherfucker. I grit my teeth until my molars ache, then scrub my palms over my unshaven face in an effort to wipe away the fog of exhaustion. I'm taking this out on the wrong person. This clusterfuck is entirely *my* fault. I shouldn't have let her out of my sight—nor gotten off the plane without our usual security measures in place. But I was arrogant. Or maybe the shock of Alina's diagnosis and the resulting lack of sleep hindered my ability to think straight. Either way, I decided Ruslan and I would be enough to keep Alina safe until our guards arrived, and I never imagined she'd be able to slip away right under my nose—especially given how sick she's been.

Or how she reached for me in that dressing room.

I push the memory away and force myself to focus. I can rage at my gullibility later. For now, I have to locate her and bring her back before it's too late.

"How could she not have been spotted?" I repeat, a tad calmer. "How much of the footage have our hackers reviewed?"

Chekhov grimaces. "All of it. The dress shop, which you already know about, is the one and only recording of her. Neither of the traffic cams at the cross streets caught her after she exited the shop. Nor did any security cameras from the nearby businesses—though, with this being an old historic area, there were quite a few shops that didn't have any cameras whatsoever, including several of the ones immediately surrounding the dress shop."

Fuck. Unless my wife has suddenly developed the skills of a professional spy, there's only one explanation for her too-thorough disappearance: her brothers have already gotten involved, specifically Konstantin with his hackers. Though I don't know why they'd bother erasing the footage from after the dress shop and not from before. Why not erase all of it instead of letting us track her for several blocks? Then again, maybe we got to that footage before they did. Either way, it's obvious what happened.

Alina saw an opportunity to run, took it, and immediately contacted her brothers—who acted swiftly to cover her digital trail, allowing her to escape unobserved to their designated rendezvous point.

I take another deep breath and try to think through the haze of fury in my brain. It's been a little over five hours since she climbed out of that window. That means she might still be somewhere in Geneva, waiting to be picked up by her brothers or whoever they're sending. I doubt the Molotovs just happened to have a trustworthy-enough crew stationed nearby, so they're probably coming from Moscow, same as my people. How much time does that give me to retrieve Alina before we have to fight a full-out battle? A few hours? More? Less?

Less, I decide. Much less. If the Molotovs tracked my plane and figured out its destination prior to us landing—which is more than likely given Konstantin's hackers' capabilities—they were already on the way here when we arrived. So I have a couple of hours at best. After that, things are going to get bloody.

"Make sure our people are stationed at every airport, public or private, within driving distance," I tell Chekhov as his phone vibrates in his hand. "If we don't find her before her brothers arrive, we'll follow them to her."

"Already on it," he says absentmindedly, looking at the screen. Suddenly, his posture changes, and his head snaps up to meet my gaze. "Our hackers located the flight plan for the Molotov jet. It's scheduled to land in four and a half hours at the same airport we used. Both Konstantin and Valery are on board."

I stare at him, taken aback. "They filed a flight plan?"

That's not like the Molotovs at all. Normally, they're very good at concealing their movements—and they'd definitely want to do that this time to avoid leading me to my runaway bride. Unless... they're sending a separate team to pick her up while we're distracted by Konstantin and Valery.

Chekhov is clearly thinking along the same lines. "It's most likely a decoy."

"I'm almost certain it is," Ruslan says, looking up from his laptop. Unlike me, who has been pacing around my newly purchased penthouse for the past hour, he's lounging on the couch, unfazed by the events. And why not? It's not *his* fucking wife who's pregnant, sick, and on the run.

I'm about to snap at him when my phone pings with an incoming email. I glance at the screen, and my pulse jolts.

It's a reply to the message I sent to the Molotovs the other day, notifying them of Alina's diagnosis.

Konstantin and I are coming to see her. Don't stand in our way.

-VM

I frown and show it to Ruslan and Chekhov.

Ruslan's frown matches mine. "Why would they warn you that they're coming? We're supposed to have figured that out on our own thanks to their supposed slip-up, right? Otherwise, it's a shitty decoy."

"They're making it sound like they don't know Alina ran away," Chekhov says, scanning the message again. "How stupid do they think we are?"

I take my phone back and read over the message. It could be interpreted that way—or it could be that they're warning me to stand aside and let them retrieve Alina without a fight. Either way, the message is out of character for Valery.

"Something's not adding up," Ruslan says, voicing my thoughts. "They have to know that we know that they're in touch with Alina. Could the message have been sent prior to her escape? Maybe there was a delay in the email reaching us for some reason?"

That's a possibility, though an unlikely one. But it's a better theory than anything else I can think of. Either way... "Tell the guards to be prepared for anything," I tell Chekhov. "And continue keeping an eye on all the other airports, along with train and bus stations. Also, set up checkpoints on all the roads leading out of Geneva. Call in every favor we've got."

"On it," he says, his thumbs already flying over his phone's screen.

I leave him to it and walk over to the window to stare out at the gleaming waters of Lake Geneva. I'd purchased this penthouse prior to Alina's escape so we'd have a place to stay during her treatment. Its proximity to the clinic and pretty views were the main selling points. Now it's going to serve as our base of operations as we search for her and prepare for war with her brothers.

"You should get some rest. This won't be resolved anytime soon," Ruslan says, coming up to stand next to me.

"I'll rest when we find her."

"No, you won't. That's when she'll need you the most. So you should get some shuteye now, while nothing is happening."

Fuck. He's right. I scrub my hand over my face again. The lack of sleep is taking a toll on me. My eyes burn with exhaustion, my muscles ache, and my thinking is slow and muddled. Worse yet, my temper is at a hair trigger. If I don't get some sleep soon, I won't just be useless—I'll be dangerous.

"Go crash for an hour or two," Ruslan says. "I'll wake you up if we find out anything."

I nod curtly and go.

IT FEELS LIKE I'VE BARELY SHUT MY EYES WHEN I'M roughly shaken awake. For a second, I'm disoriented, but then the events of the past couple of days flood my brain and I jackknife off the bed, nearly knocking Ruslan off his feet as I grab for my phone to check the time.

Fuck. It's nearly six hours later. I should've set a fucking alarm instead of trusting my brother to wake me.

"Did we find her?" I demand, stuffing the phone into my pocket.

"No." Ruslan's expression is strangely tight. "Her brothers are here, though."

"You mean they've landed?"

"I mean, they're fucking *here*, in your living room."

I shoot him a disbelieving look before stalking out into said living room. Sure enough, Konstantin and Valery Molotov are sitting on my couch, identical hazel-gold eyes trained on me with undisguised hostility.

What the fuck?

"They came by themselves," Ruslan says in a low voice before I can approach our uninvited guests. "I had them searched for weapons before letting them in. They're clean. And I think… they don't know where Alina is either."

My right hand clenches into a fist. "Bullshit."

"Just hear them out," Ruslan says under his breath. "If it's an act, it's a fucking good one."

I fight the urge to deck him, or better yet, both of Alina's brothers. Instead, I call upon every ounce of restraint and approach the couch.

They stand as I stop in front of them. It's eerie how

alike they look, despite being nearly six years apart in age and Konstantin wearing glasses. They're almost like twins. Or triplets, if you count their middle brother, Nikolai—who, it appears, couldn't make it to the party. Probably because he's busy playing daddy to *my* nephew.

It sets my teeth on edge just thinking about it.

The two Molotovs match me in height, so we're eye to eye as we glare at each other.

Valery breaks the silence first. His voice is like a shard of glass in winter. "I told you not to stand in our way, Leonov. We came unarmed—now let us see her."

It's hard to keep my face expressionless. "You want to see your sister."

"That's right," Konstantin says, his tone calm despite the hatred burning in his eyes. "Your email said she'll be undergoing surgery shortly. We want to see her before she goes under the knife."

This is fucking weird. Are they here as a diversion? Do they think we'll call off our men and stop looking for Alina if they pretend like they know nothing? If so, that's a very risky ploy. The full contingent of my guards is here now, so I could have them both detained. I could keep them prisoner and torture them until they tell me exactly where Alina is. Alina wouldn't appreciate it if I killed them, so I'll try not to, but they wouldn't have to know that.

Then again, they undoubtedly have their men stationed nearby, ready to attempt a rescue if needed. Maybe they think that's assurance enough, and this game is worth it. But to what end? Why take this kind of risk for a not-so-convincing ploy?

I have to find out, which means playing along for now.

"She's resting," I say coolly. "I'll tell her you're here when she wakes up."

Valery's jaw hardens. "We'll see her *now*."

Yeah, sure. "How did you find us?" I ask, as if he hasn't spoken.

"We tracked your plane," Konstantin replies flatly. "From there, it wasn't hard to figure out which penthouse you'd purchased. There were only a few on the market in Geneva, and only one was bought by an untraceable shell company. I'm sure you knew that, though."

So I did. And they knew that I knew they'd be coming. So why the hell are they pretending like I don't know Alina would reach out to them first thing?

Unless… she didn't. Or couldn't.

Everything inside me goes cold.

What if she didn't climb out of that window on her own?

What if someone took her?

Fuck knows, her brothers and I have enemies to spare.

Goddammit. What if that's what the Molotovs want me to think so they can get her out of Geneva without bloodshed? Is this what they're hoping to achieve by coming here unarmed—convincing me that they're not involved in her disappearance?

Then again, what if they aren't?

"We'll see her *now*," Valery repeats harshly, taking a step forward, and Konstantin does the same. Their faces are hard, determined, their postures tense and combat ready—the very picture of brothers dead set on getting to their sick sister, regardless of the risk to themselves.

Ruslan was right. If it's a fucking act, it's an Oscar-worthy one.

The threat of violence hangs in the air, thickening the atmosphere, and I make a split-second decision. Because the only thing worse than Alina's brothers taking her from me would be someone else doing that. Someone who doesn't care for her.

Someone who wants to hurt me or her brothers through her.

"I don't have her," I say, laying all the cards on the table. "And the two of you either know that full well, or she's in big fucking trouble."

CHAPTER 5

ALINA

I writhe on the bed, the pain in my skull unbearable, nauseating. In the past, I've had drugs —migraine meds, painkillers, or pot—to help me through these episodes. But I don't dare take so much as a Tylenol now, not when I have yet to decide what to do about the fragile life inside me.

My baby girl. She's still only the size of a speck of lint, and I already love her.

"Come on, let me get you something," Birgit begs as she presents the bucket for me to be sick in for the umpteenth time. "Or let me take you to a hospital."

"No," I groan when I'm done heaving. "Please don't. You… you promised."

She nods, but she looks unsure. Probably because it's one thing to impulsively offer to help a stranger, but it's something else entirely to play nursemaid to said stranger for two days straight. At least I think it's been two days. I've been fading in and out of consciousness, the agony in my head crowding out my awareness of anything but the pain.

And it's not getting better. It won't get better unless I take the drugs. And maybe not even then. Because there's a tumor in my head, growing and spreading with each passing moment.

Now that I know it's there, I can feel it. The dizziness, the nausea—it's worse than it's ever been. Each time Birgit helps me to the bathroom, I am less steady on my feet. I've been seeing white specks in front of my eyes, and Birgit told me I shook uncontrollably a few hours ago, as if from a seizure.

Probably because it *was* a seizure.

I can't go on like this, I know that, but I don't know what to do.

Return to Alexei? Call my brothers? I can't think through this pain.

I do know that I need to make a decision soon. I can't keep letting Birgit take care of me. Not that she will do it for much longer. With each hour that passes without me getting better, she looks more worried. Promise or not, she'll call an ambulance or force me to go to a hospital soon.

I'm also worried. Not about myself but about the baby. All I've been able to eat in the past two days is a slice of dry toast, and I threw that up. Today, I threw up from just a few sips of water, and I haven't needed to pee in forever. That's bad. It means I'm getting dehydrated. If this continues, I'll have no choice but to seek medical attention and thus bring myself to Alexei's attention—assuming he's looking, that is.

The fact that he hasn't found me yet may be a sign that he isn't.

I struggle to think through the crushing pain in my skull. I know he has a team of hackers on call, same as my brothers. If it's been two days, that's definitely long enough for them to access traffic cams, security footage, and whatever else they use to track down people. By now, he must know where I am… unless he doesn't care to know.

Unless he doesn't want me.

Maybe he's realized he's better off without me.

Maybe he's always enjoyed the chase, and when I reached for him in that dressing room of my own accord, I killed his desire for me.

My empty stomach twists and churns as I squeeze my eyes shut and huddle deeper into the thin blanket, so miserable I want to die.

No, that's wrong. I want to live.

I want that little speck inside me to grow and flourish.

I want to see my daughter, even if it costs me everything.

And… I want Alexei.

I want to feel his arms around me, to burrow into the warm crook of his neck and breathe in his masculine scent. I want it so badly I ache with it, even though it doesn't make any sense.

All I've ever wanted is freedom from him, and now

that I have it, all I can think about is going back into his cage.

————

I MUST DRIFT OFF FOR A BIT BECAUSE WHEN I OPEN MY eyes next time, it's dark, and I'm a little bit less sick. Birgit is nowhere to be found—probably went out for dinner and drinks. I vaguely recall her talking about getting asked out by some guy on a dating app. The two other beds in the room are empty as well, which doesn't surprise me. The two Italian girls checked out yesterday, and I guess this hostel is not that popular.

I don't know what woke me. As far as I can tell, I still don't have to pee, nor am I particularly nauseated, though I'm still quite dizzy. Maybe I'm thirsty? I push up onto my elbow and reach for a glass of water Birgit thoughtfully left for me on the nightstand.

And that's when I see it.

A shadow.

It steps out of the corner of the room, and the dim light seeping in through the window reveals a man's silhouette.

A big man's silhouette.

My first thought is that it's Alexei.

He's found me.

Wild, irrational joy surges through me—only to dissolve into icy panic as I catch a whiff of cheap cologne, tobacco, and alcohol.

As I realize there's a stranger in my hostel room.

CHAPTER 6

ALEXEI

If anyone ever told me I'd be collaborating with the Molotov brothers, I'd tell them to check themselves for psychosis. Yet here we are, Valery, Konstantin, and I, huddled over a laptop at night, reviewing the latest discovery from our teams of hackers—who, like us, are actually working together.

They've been able to reconstruct Alina's movements up to the point of her exiting the dress shop and have confirmed that no further footage exists. The surrounding cameras haven't been tampered with, like I originally thought.

My wife simply didn't show up in any cameras after she stepped out of that fucking shop and took a few steps down the street.

"If an abduction happened, it would've had to take place right here," Konstantin says, drawing a red circle on the map on the screen. "A dozen feet south, it would've been within the range of several cameras. A few feet north, same thing."

Valery peers at the screen. "There's an alley right in that blind spot."

I've already spotted the same thing. "That's where a kidnapper could've been hiding." My voice is as tight as my ribcage. I haven't been able to take a full breath since I realized that Alina's brothers aren't here as some convoluted ploy to throw me off her scent. Nor have I been able to eat or sleep.

It took a while to convince the Molotovs that this is not a ploy on *my* part to keep them away from Alina, and once they finally accepted that, we got down to business and have been working nonstop, deploying all our contacts and connections to figure out which of our enemies may have been behind this.

Unfortunately, between us and the Molotovs, there are many, many suspects.

"I'll send a forensic team to that alley first thing in the morning," Valery says, pulling out his phone. "We'll see if they find any signs of struggle."

"Good idea," I say and straighten. "In the meantime, I'm heading there myself."

Konstantin looks up from the screen, his eyes glinting behind his glasses. "Why? You'll just tamper with potential evidence."

I bare my teeth at him. "I'm not a fucking idiot. I'll be careful."

"I'll go with you," Ruslan says, rising from the couch where he was working on his own laptop.

I glower at him, having all but forgotten about his presence. I have no idea why he's here instead of in his bed, asleep. He's certainly no fan of the Molotovs, and he hasn't been actively participating in the search for Alina, focusing instead on matters back home.

Matters like our father. Who's dying and sending daily demands to see us.

I shove the thought aside. That's the last thing I want to worry about now. "Let's go then," I tell Ruslan curtly and walk over to grab my gun from a nearby table. I stuff it into my belt and cover it with my shirt. My knife is already strapped to my ankle inside my boot, and I have a smaller-caliber gun strapped to my other ankle. But I make a show of getting the weapon anyway, for the Molotovs' sake. I don't want them knowing that I've been armed this whole time—though they probably suspect it.

Temporary collaboration or not, we trust each other about as much as two hungry gators around a rabbit.

"I'll come too," Valery says, smoothly rising to his feet.

I grit my teeth, having looked forward to a Molotov-free hour. It's not worth antagonizing Alina's brother, though, so I keep silent as he follows Ruslan and me out of the penthouse. I know he still suspects me of some ploy, just as, on some level, I suspect him and Konstantin of the same.

The alley is not far, so we walk there on foot. Behind us, some half a block away, several of my men trail us unobtrusively, as do a few of the Molotovs' guards. They're not as subtle as my guys, whom I've chosen specifically for the purpose of discreetly keeping an eye on Alina over the years. Either way, if shit goes down, we're well prepared. Not that anything is likely to go down. If Alina did get taken, it was by someone who's highly skilled at covering their tracks, and the odds of us finding anything—much less encountering anyone—in that alley are minuscule.

"Just how sick is she?" Valery asks, breaking the tense silence.

His voice is cool, unruffled, as if he couldn't give a fuck about the answer, but the fact that he asked tells me he's worried. Which is somewhat surprising. Over my years of following Alina, I've compiled dossiers on all of her friends and relatives, and by all indications, her youngest brother fits the clinical definition of a sociopath, complete with a lack of emotions and a highly manipulative nature. Though, to be fair, people have said that about me as well.

Regardless, I slant a suspicious glance at him, and so does Ruslan.

"Why?" I ask bluntly.

"Because she's my sister, and I want to know how she is."

Logical. Yet… "You haven't asked about her state before. Why now?"

With a different man, I could chalk this up to small talk, but Valery Molotov doesn't make small talk.

Everything he says and does has a purpose, however convoluted that purpose may be.

"Because there's something you're not telling us." Valery's tone is even as we turn the corner onto the street where Alina was last spotted. "Something important. What is it?"

He's right. I haven't told them anything about Alina's pregnancy—because that's between me and Alina. More importantly, it has no bearing on anything.

"She's very sick," I say, ignoring his second question. "She's dizzy, weak, nauseated, has headaches. Pretty much what you'd expect with fucking brain cancer. What else do you want to know?"

"Did you hurt her?" His voice is still level, his expression unreadable as he glances at me. "Is that why she ran even though she's so sick?"

So that's where he's heading. My molars squeeze together, hard. "I would never fucking hurt her."

"Then why would she run before a life-saving surgery? Unless being with you is so unbearable that she'd rather die."

It's all I can do not to reach for my knife right here, in the middle of a street that's still crowded despite the late hour. I have to take several deep breaths to control myself, and still, when my voice emerges, it's harsh and guttural. "You don't know what the fuck you're talking about. She *wants* me. She—" I stop because as much as I want to say that she loves me, I know that's not the case. Not yet.

I need more time with her.

I need to show her that we belong together.

"Sure she does." Valery's tone is cool and mocking. "That's why she avoided you all those years. Because she wants you so fucking much."

If he weren't Alina's brother, he'd already be bleeding out on the pavement. As is, something of what I'm feeling must show on my face because he says matter-of-factly, "You know, a sniper of mine has the two of you in his sights."

Ruslan catches my gaze, and I nod subtly, giving him my go-ahead. He pulls out his phone, and a second later, a red dot appears on Valery's chest and travels up his face before settling on his forehead.

Alina's brother stops and meets my gaze, a cold smirk tugging at his lips. "Touché."

We have a whole team of snipers stationed in this area, ready to take out the Molotovs and their crew if they make the wrong move. I'm not surprised that they implemented the same measures. Nor will I be surprised if, after we find Alina, our temporary collaboration devolves into the bloodiest battle between our families yet.

But for now, we're allies. Because we have to find her and soon. I can't stop thinking about Alina sick and hurt, in the hands of some enemy who sees her as nothing but a tool to be used to gain an edge over me or her brothers. My stomach feels like it's being clawed to shreds from the inside as I keep picturing the way her abduction could've gone down, how they could've violently subdued her or drugged her. Or...

No. I refuse to think that they could've killed her. That would not benefit anyone.

Except an enemy who wants the ultimate revenge.

I shut down that thought before it can unravel me completely. Reining in my fury at Alina's brother, I resume walking swiftly, and Ruslan follows my lead. As Valery falls into step next to us, I ask in as steady a voice as I can manage, "Any theories on why we haven't been contacted yet?"

"They're buying themselves time to set up the most advantageous exchange," Valery answers immediately. "The psychological torment inflicted on us as a result is an added bonus."

Of course he's already thought this through. I would have as well if I weren't so fucking sleep deprived. Not to mention, furious and terrified.

If Alina did get taken, whoever has her will pay a price they couldn't have imagined. No matter how much they plan and plot, I will find them, and I will obliterate them and everything they've ever known and loved.

Spotting the turn to the alley, I quicken my pace. Ruslan and Valery do the same. The tourists we pass wisely move out of our way.

I step into the alley first. At a glance, it's nothing extraordinary. Small and narrow, it houses a dumpster and not much else. There is a faint odor of trash and urine—drunk tourists likely relieve themselves here— and I spot a semi-dry puddle of something that looks like old vomit on the cobblestones near the dumpster.

It's likely from the drunk tourists as well. Then again... I turn to Valery. "Tell your forensic team to get that"—I point at the puddle—"tested for DNA. Alina's been getting sick a lot."

He nods and pulls out his phone to fire off the message. In the meantime, Ruslan and I advance deeper into the alley, using our phones as flashlights to scan the ground and the walls. I'm looking for blood, scuff marks from shoes, strands of hair—anything that could provide a clue as to what happened to my wife.

Which is why when my gaze lands on the door in the middle of the wall, it takes me a second to register what I'm seeing.

Ruslan is already there, ahead of me. "Why didn't we know about this?" he asks, touching the worn wood of the frame.

Frowning, I approach. "Because this door isn't supposed to be here."

According to the schematics of the nearby buildings that our hackers found, there should be nothing on these walls except a couple of small windows on the second, third, and fourth floors.

"This door could've been added after the building was built," Valery says, appearing at my elbow. "I imagine the residents found it convenient to have more than one exit. If I recall correctly, this is currently a hostel."

A hostel.

My heartbeat picks up pace.

Why the fuck didn't we consider this possibility before?

A hostel is a place where a person—say, a stubborn wife on the run—could easily stay for a couple of days, no abduction required.

"Let's go in," Ruslan says, but I'm already there, turning the handle.

I expect the door to be locked, but it opens easily, revealing a small lounge with shabby furniture. On the wall to my right is a small, empty reception desk and a set of doors that likely lead out to the main street. To my left, in the far corner, is a spiral staircase.

Valery is already heading over to the stairs, but I beat him there. Anticipation hums in my veins as I take the stairs three at a time.

I can all but feel her nearby, can sense her nearness in some uncanny way.

Clearing the stairs, I end up in a narrow hallway with three doors.

I push one open.

It's a bathroom.

The second door reveals a row of showers.

Holding my breath, I approach the third.

As I reach for the handle, a sound reaches my ears.

A low, muffled female sob.

Everything inside me turns to ice even as adrenaline explodes in my veins.

My gun is already in my hand as I kick open the door—and freeze, stunned by the bloody scene before me.

Chapter 7

Alina

My first instinct is to scream. But I don't. Nobody would hear me, and though I've never had an opportunity to use my self-defense training, I remember what Pavel taught me.

Grabbing the glass of water I was reaching for, I throw myself off the bed on the opposite side of where the unknown man is standing.

It must hurt when my hip and shoulder hit the floor, but I don't feel it. Just as I don't feel the dizziness and the nausea that have been my constant companions of late. The adrenaline surging through me is like an infusion of espresso directly into my veins. My mind is crystal clear as I keep rolling, the glass clutched firmly in my hand. Behind me, I hear the intruder utter a vile French curse before his heavy footsteps round the bed.

I spring to my feet like a pop-up toy, the adrenaline lending me an athlete's strength. In a split second, I take in my surroundings, searching for any potential avenues of escape.

There are none.

The intruder is between me and the door, and I wouldn't be able to open the ancient window in time. Plus, we're on the second floor.

I either go through him, or he corners me.

He must still think I'm helpless because he lets out a low, drunk laugh and lumbers toward me. "Pretty, pretty kitty," he croons in French. "Come to papa, pretty girl. Come on, let me pet you…"

I clench my teeth and clutch the glass harder.

I recognize that voice now. I heard it downstairs a few times as I lay here sick.

It's the hostel owner's son. "A pervy idiot" according to Birgit. Though she also said that he's harmless. I guess she was wrong about that, or she's never seen him drunk.

Either way, I'm going to give him a chance to leave of his own accord.

Pitching my voice low and hard, I channel Alexei. "Get the fuck out. Now."

He laughs drunkenly and comes toward me. "Here, kitty, kitty, kitty…"

I can tell he expects me to back away until I'm caught against the wall, so I do the exact opposite.

I throw myself at him, launching forward with the glass clutched tightly in my outstretched hand. It crashes against his skull, and pain stabs my palm as the thick glass breaks, puncturing my hand. Ignoring the hot wash of blood, I hold on to the shard that remains in my grip and jump to the side as the man reels back, cursing and clutching his head.

There's now half a meter of space between him and the path to the door. I could try to make a run for it. But if he grabs me, I won't make it.

He'll drag me down and use his heavy bulk to pin me.

All this runs through my brain in a nanosecond. Later, I will wonder if there was another way. I will question whether what I'm about to do was the only way to protect myself and the baby, or if it was just my Molotov blood showing its true colors.

For now, though, I simply act.

Before the man can regroup, I attack, sweeping the shard of glass in a wide, vicious arc, aiming for a disabling strike across his neck.

My aim is stunningly accurate despite the dim light.

I feel the sharp glass bite into soft tissue and hear the gurgle as he drops to his knees, clutching at his throat.

Panting, I back away as more gurgling sounds fill the room. And then... then he falls, and there's only silence.

I keep backing away until my shoulders touch a wall. Shakily, I feel along said wall until I find the light switch by the door.

The shard of glass is still in my hand as I flip the switch to illuminate the room... and see the man lying in a pool of blood.

The man I just murdered.

My knees buckle, and the shard falls out of my numb fingers as I sink to the floor, gasping. No matter how much air I suck in, I can't seem to get enough oxygen. My vision darkens as I struggle against the iron bands that suddenly seem to encase my lungs.

I must pass out. Or maybe I simply wish I had. Some part of me is cognizant of the sobs trying to force their way out of my closed throat and the icy chill rendering my fingers and toes numb and useless. That same part knows that I need to get up and go. To leave the scene of the crime before it's too late.

Only I can't move. I can only stare at the man I slaughtered. A human being whose life I mercilessly ended.

I'm just like my father.

And Nikolai.

And Alexei.

Maybe it's because I'm thinking of him, or maybe I'm simply in shock, but when something crashes into the door and it flies open, revealing my husband's dark figure, I can't help but think that I've conjured him up. That he's not real but a hallucination, a demonic phantasm I've willed into existence in my hour of need.

And maybe that's why when he reaches for me, I fall into his embrace, sobbing and grateful to be there.

To be back where I belong.

Chapter 8

Alexei

As Alina buries her face in the crook of my neck and loops her arms around my waist, I reflexively squeeze her against me in a fierce, joyous hug. Immediately, I loosen my embrace. For all I know, she could be hurt, injured. I need to let go of her so I can examine her, but she's crying and shaking, uneven sobs wracking her slim frame as she clings to me, and I can't make myself pull away because I'm fucking trembling myself.

What the fuck did I just walk in on?

Why is there so much blood on her hands and dress?

Who is the dead man on the floor?

If he hurt my Alinyonok in any way, I'll fucking kill him all over again. Him and—

"Is she okay? Give her to me."

Fuck. Valery. I've forgotten all about him and Ruslan.

Alina doesn't seem to have registered his presence yet, so I turn with her in my arms, keeping her back to Valery, and mouth to Ruslan, "Get rid of him."

My brother nods and steps in front of Valery. "Let's give them space." His tone makes it clear it's not a suggestion.

Valery ignores it regardless. His voice is pure ice as he demands, "That is my fucking sister. Move aside. Now."

Alina lifts her head off my shoulder and wedges her hands between us, pushing with all her might. Reluctantly, I let her turn around, though I keep one arm locked around her ribcage.

"Valery?" She sounds incredulous. "What are you…" Her gaze shifts between Ruslan and her brother before she glances up at me with a confused expression.

"Are you okay?" I ask, ignoring the unspoken question on her face. "Did that fucker hurt you?" I drop my arm and turn her to face me so I can finally examine her. Gently, I run my hands over her, looking for any injuries that might not have been apparent at first glance. All I find is a deep gash across her right palm. It's still bleeding and will likely need at least a dozen stitches.

"We have to get you to a doctor," I say as I rip at the hem of my shirt. "For now, close your fist around this and hold tight." I tie the strip of material around her palm and close her fingers for good measure.

She blinks up at me, her jade eyes swimming with fresh tears. "Alexei…" Her voice shakes. "I killed him."

"I figured as much." I meet Valery's coldly furious gaze across Ruslan's shoulder. "You hear that, Molotov? You might want to tell your forensic team to hurry up and get here ASAP—unless you want me to call in my guys."

Valery's mouth flattens. "My people will take care of it. Now give me my sister. Alina, step away from him."

Not a fat chance in hell. I grip her arm and pull her against me as she turns to look at her brother. "She's not going anywhere."

Valery makes what seems like the smallest movement, yet suddenly, there's a gun in his outstretched hand, pointing straight at Ruslan.

I clench my teeth, equal parts pissed and reluctantly impressed.

He's fast with a weapon. Maybe as fast as I am. Also, so much for frisking him and his brother at my penthouse. Like me, he's been armed all along and hiding it.

"Step away from her," he repeats grimly, and I make a show of letting go of Alina so I can ostensibly get my weapon—but really to provide a distraction for my brother.

The ploy works. With Valery's attention on me for a split second, Ruslan yanks out his knife and sends it flying at Valery's face.

Once again, the fucker moves fast, ducking to the side so the blade just grazes his cheekbone.

"Stop!"

Alina's high-pitched yell freezes me in my tracks. It

has the same effect on Valery, though not Ruslan, who uses this new distraction to pull out his gun and aim it at Valery's head.

I grab Alina and pull her behind me in case bullets start flying.

"Stop this madness!" she yells again, trying to push me aside. "Valery, back off!"

I don't budge an inch, continuing to shield her even as her brother reluctantly lowers his weapon. He's realized he's unlikely to win this fight now, at least not without putting his sister in grave danger.

"That's right, Molotov, back off," I say, unable to stop myself from rubbing it in. "Get the fuck out of here and call Konstantin, update him on our lucky find. In the meantime, I'll take my *wife*"—I emphasize the word—"back to the clinic."

What I really want is for both of Alina's brothers to get on a plane back to Moscow, but that's unlikely to happen. They'll want to be here for Alina's surgery—and for the chance to steal her from me. But they won't be able to do that, not as long as I'm prepared. That's why I notified them of Alina's diagnosis while we were on the way to the clinic: because I knew they'd be coming for us as soon as we left the yacht, and it was better that they understood the situation before they did something to get in the way of Alina's treatment.

Also, if it were my sister, I'd want to know.

"Yes, go, Valery," Alina says from behind me, her voice a tad calmer. "Please."

Her brother stares at me for a long, tense moment, then pockets his gun. "All right. I will see you soon."

It's as much a threat to me as it is a promise to her.

"Yes, you will," I say coolly. "As long as you and Konstantin behave."

He turns and leaves. Ruslan walks out after him, leaving us alone with the dead body.

I need to know what happened, but first, I need to get Alina out of here, far away from all the blood and death. Her face is a pale shade of green as she turns to stare at the corpse, so I don't waste time asking her any questions. Unceremoniously, I pick her up and carry her out of the room and down the stairs to the hostel lobby, and then out to the alley, where I message our men to come and get us in a car.

I can't have anyone see us while she's in this state, not with the fresh body we've left behind.

"Wait," Alina says shakily as the car I ordered pulls up to the alley's entrance. "Birgit. I have to tell her…"

Fuck. I stop and carefully lower Alina to her feet. "Who's Birgit?"

If there was a witness—

"Just a girl," Alina says, and her lower lip wobbles as she stares up at me. "She helped me when I was feeling sick."

"Was she there?" I ask softly.

Alina's answering stare is blank. She must still be in shock.

I soften my tone further, speaking as if to a small child. "When the bad man died, was she there?"

Comprehension flares in her gaze, followed by fear. "No! No, she was nowhere near. I just want to let her know that I'm leaving; otherwise, she'll worry and wonder. Alexei…" She grabs my hand with both of hers and squeezes with surprising strength. Her jade eyes are dark in her pale face. "Don't hurt her. Promise me you won't hurt her."

I sigh. "Alinyonok…"

"Promise me!"

How evil does she think I am? "I won't hurt her."

Not unless I find out she hurt Alina or was somehow responsible for the dead man being in her room. But I keep those qualifiers to myself.

Alina relaxes a tiny bit and releases my hand. "Okay. Let me go leave her a note then."

She moves to walk around me, but I step to the side to block her way. She's clearly not thinking straight.

"That's not a good idea," I say as gently as I can.

Her eyes narrow, then widen. "Oh. Of course. I just—"

"I'm sure your brother's team will do a good job of cleaning up the scene, but it's still best if there are no traces of your presence there," I say, pulling her into my embrace as she begins to visibly shake again. Softly, I add into her hair, "You can contact Birgit later, once everything settles down." Or preferably, never. Either way, I'll need to do a deep dive on this Birgit's background, just in case.

Keeping Alina pressed against me, I guide her into the back seat of the car, where I pull her onto my lap and let her bury her face in my shoulder while I stroke her hair, feeling her trembling slowly subside.

I have a million questions, but I allow myself to ask only one. "Was there anyone else besides Birgit who helped you or stayed with you?" I keep my tone light and conversational, as if it doesn't matter.

"No." Alina's answer is swift as she raises her head. Her face is wet with tears, but her gaze is clear and direct. And more than a little fearful. "Alexei, there was no one else. And definitely no witnesses to..." She swallows audibly. "To what I did."

She seems more with it now, less shock-y, so I decide to risk a couple more questions. "Who was he?" I ask carefully. "What was he doing there?"

The sooner I learn what happened, the better our odds of covering up the scene.

She swallows again, her slim throat working as she moves off me to sit on the seat. "I don't know for sure, but I think he might be—" Her voice breaks. "That is, might've been the hostel owner's son. I'd never seen him before, but I'd heard his voice downstairs a few times. Birgit said he doesn't bother the girls usually, not unless they flirt with him, but—"

"He decided to bother you." It takes all my self-control to keep my voice steady as white-hot rage scorches my chest. I'd suspected something like that to be the case, but to hear her confirm it... "Did he hurt you?" Despite my best efforts, my voice tightens. "Alinyonok, if he—"

"No. He didn't even lay a finger on me." Her eyes

take on a haunted look. "I killed him before he could do anything. He was in the room when I woke up, and then he started saying some pervy shit. Pavel's training kicked in, and I just… acted. I didn't even try to scare him off, or talk to him, or—"

Thank fuck for Pavel. "You did the right thing. That motherfucker was more than double your size. If he'd gotten his hands on you, you wouldn't have been able to fight him off, and you knew that."

"Did I?" Her tone is hollow. "I could've just wounded him. Or tried to get past him and—"

I press my index finger to her lips, stopping her words. "Alinyonok…" My tone is as gentle as I can make it. "Even if you'd left him alive, do you honestly think he would've lived for long?"

She sucks in an audible breath. She must not have considered it until now, the fact that the moment her attacker appeared in her room, he was a dead man. If she hadn't killed him, I would have—and my method wouldn't have been nearly as quick and merciful. Especially if he'd hurt her.

Fuck, if he had hurt her… My chest tightens agonizingly.

I should've been there. I should've protected her.

No, what the fuck am I saying? She should've never been in that situation in the first place. From now on, she's going to be no farther than an arm's length from me at all times, even if I have to literally chain her to me.

The car comes to a stop, and I realize we're

already in front of the clinic. "We're here," I say unnecessarily as Alina turns around to look out the window.

Swiftly, I exit on my side, then go around to open the door for Alina and help her out. Her hand is cold and clammy in mine as she climbs out of the car, and she still seems shaky on her feet, so I sweep her up into a bridal carry and bring her inside, ignoring her protests that she can walk on her own.

Even if she were at a hundred percent, I'd want to carry her. After the hell of the past two days, holding her and feeling her warm body pressed against me is the only way I can reassure myself that she's really here, that I'm not dreaming this in an exhausted stupor.

My men already gave the clinic a heads up that we were coming, so despite the late hour, a young male nurse is there to greet us.

"The doctors are on their way," he informs us before directing me to take Alina into one of the examination rooms.

"Wait," Alina says as I carefully set her on the table in a sitting position. "I need the bathroom."

"There's one right here," the nurse says helpfully, pointing to the other door in the room. "You go ahead, and I'll be right back."

He hurries out of the room, and Alina hops off the table, all but running to the bathroom. She's about to close the door when I catch the handle and walk in after her, then shut the door behind me.

She turns with a startled expression. "Alexei? What the hell?"

I fold my arms over my chest and lean my back against the door. "Go ahead. Do what you have to do."

If she thinks I'm going to fall for the same trick twice, she's very much mistaken. Not that this bathroom even has a window, but still.

I wasn't joking about arm's length.

Some of the pallor leaves her face as a flush creeps up her neck, turning her porcelain skin blotchy in parts. "Are you insane? I'm not doing 'what I have to do' in front of you."

"Why not? We're married, and I'm not squeamish."

She snorts and crosses her arms over her chest, mimicking my stance. "Well, I am. I'm not doing anything if you're here."

We stare at each other, neither willing to compromise, until a strange expression crosses her face. She swallows, and I see all the color leach from her skin.

My heart rate spikes, and I push away from the door, instinctively reaching for her. "What is it?" I grip her shoulders. "Are you okay?"

She twists out of my hold. Her voice is thick, her face back to its greenish tint. "Can you at least turn around?"

Fuck. "Okay." I reluctantly step back and turn around, facing the door. "Just let me know if you need help, okay?"

I expect to hear retching sounds, but there's only the quiet rustle of a skirt being lifted. And then…

"Alexei."

I'm already turning around, reaching for her as she sways on her feet, her eyes brimming with tears as the skirt of her dress falls into place.

"I'm bleeding," she whispers, staring up at me. "Alexei, the baby… I'm fucking bleeding."

Chapter 9

Alina

The next couple of hours are a blur. A bunch of doctors show up, my hand is sewn up and bandaged, my blood is drawn, and an MRI scan is run. Valery and Konstantin come and argue with Alexei and Ruslan about who gets to take me and where. It's an argument they must lose because I stay at the clinic, with Alexei grimly hovering over me at all times, even when I'm finally forced to return to the bathroom to empty my painfully full bladder with him present (but at least turned away).

And the entire time, I'm bleeding. Not heavily, about the same as when my period first arrives, but there's definitely blood where there's supposed to be none.

I'm also cramping. That's what alerted me to look at my underwear in the bathroom. A sudden dull, pulsing ache low in my belly, one that's steadily worsening as the minutes tick by.

"It'll be all right," Alexei says for the tenth time, but I can tell he doesn't believe it any more than I do as we sit in the exam room with our hands joined, waiting for the lab results to confirm what I already know in my heart.

Finally, Dr. Fasseau walks in. Judging by the guarded expression on his face, he doesn't have good news.

"Mrs. Leonov," he says quietly, looking at me. "We've run your blood results, and your HCG levels are below the threshold that would indicate a pregnancy."

"What does that mean?" Alexei's tone is sharp as his hand tightens on mine. "Was there an error before? Was she never pregnant?"

"That's one possibility," Fasseau says. "But I've spoken to Dr. Bureva and a couple of my other Ob-Gyn colleagues, and they think your wife experienced what's known as a chemical pregnancy—a very early type of miscarriage. It's thought that up to fifty percent of all conceptions end this way, before a woman even knows she's pregnant. The only sign might be a delayed period."

I stare at him numbly. "Mine wasn't delayed." In fact, given today's date that I glimpsed on Alexei's phone, it's right on time.

"Right." Fasseau nods sympathetically. "Your pregnancy ended particularly early, which is a good thing, all things considered. Dr. Bureva said to expect slightly heavier-than-usual bleeding and cramping, but otherwise, it should be just like a regular period for you."

"I want to speak to Bureva," Alexei says, his tone brooking no argument. "Get her on the phone for us, now."

Fasseau must've expected the demand because he's already swiping across his screen. A moment later, he hands us the phone, which Alexei puts on speaker as soon as he hears the Ob-Gyn's voice. He fires off a bunch of questions at her, most of them having to do with how I'll be feeling and whether it's safe to proceed with the surgery and the cancer treatment. I only half listen to the answers, too numb to process more than a few words here and there.

My baby girl.

She's gone.

She never truly existed.

"—the most likely explanation is a chromosomal abnormality," Bureva is saying when I finally manage to tune back in. "The blastocyst was unable to develop normally, and the implantation did not progress—hence only a brief elevation in your HCG levels. If not for the blood test, you probably would've never known you'd conceived, as your wife would've gotten her period on time."

A brief elevation.

I squeeze my eyes shut to stop the tears burning them from escaping. My baby girl never got to the size of the speck of lint I had imagined. She never progressed beyond a few cells, her very existence a blip, a "brief elevation" I wouldn't have known about if not for the tumor growing in my brain, mimicking pregnancy symptoms.

There's no decision to be made now. There never was, as it turns out.

I should be glad. Relieved. If I proceed with the treatment, I won't be ending my baby girl's life. If I understand what Bureva is saying, she never stood a chance. So why does this feel like I've lost something real and precious?

"Is it because I'm sick?" I swallow the burning knot in my throat and open my eyes. "Is that why the chromosomes were abnormal?"

"Not necessarily," Bureva replies. "Nobody knows why this happens, though certain medical conditions, like thyroid disorders and diabetes, do make it more likely, as does conception past the age of thirty-five. But perfectly healthy young women experience chemical pregnancies as well. It's incredibly common, and most women go on to carry healthy babies in the future." She pauses. "In your case, I would suggest harvesting your eggs prior to embarking on more aggressive forms of treatment—that is, if the timeline Dr. Fasseau and his colleagues have in mind allows it."

"We will have a better idea about that after the surgery," Fasseau says. "So far, the MRI scan you've just undergone confirms the findings of the portable MRI used by Dr. Kressler."

Of course it does. A violent swell of nausea makes me pull my hand out of Alexei's grip and bring it to my mouth.

"Excuse me," I mutter, shakily getting up. "I need a minute."

Alexei is already on his feet. "Let's go."

He comes with me to the bathroom, and I'm too sick and miserable to force him out. It's all I can do to make it to the toilet bowl in time to empty my stomach contents into it instead of onto the floor. By the time I stop heaving, I'm sweating and shaking, and he's right there beside me, holding my hair, helping me to my feet, guiding me to the sink to wash my face and rinse out my mouth.

When it's all over, I feel so embarrassed that I want to die. But Alexei doesn't look the least bit fazed. Instead, he guides me out of the bathroom, sits me down next to him, and dives right back into the conversation with the doctors, holding my hand clasped in his the entire time.

Once again, I only half listen as they discuss the specifics of the MRI findings and the various treatment protocols and timelines. My head is pounding, my stomach is still churning, and I'm so drained that I could pass out right here and now, no bed required. Though I do my best to stay upright, I find myself slumping more and more against Alexei, until he says, "Let's continue this later. Alina needs her rest."

Fasseau nods, stifling a yawn. "As do we all. We'll schedule the surgery for noon, to make sure everybody is fresh and ready." Then, likely recalling that he's dealing with a dangerous man, he adds cautiously, "That is, if that's okay with you."

Alexei nods grimly and gets up, pulling me to my feet. "We'll be here at noon."

And picking me up over my objections, he carries me out of the clinic and across the street to his penthouse, where I fall asleep the moment he lays me down on his bed.

CHAPTER 10

ALEXEI

She's asleep. Here. In my bed.

Holding my breath, I touch her. I can't help myself. I need to make sure that she's real, that this isn't a dream caused by my involuntary passing out from lack of sleep. But no. Her jet-black hair is soft and silky as I brush my hand over it, the skin of her bare arm supple and warm.

I exhale raggedly and pull my hand away, not wanting to wake her. Then I realize she's still wearing the dress she ran away in, the same blood-stained dress I found her in at the hostel. It definitely needs to be changed. Gently, I roll her onto her side and use my knife to slice through the material in the front and back so I can remove it without disturbing her too much. As I do so, I try my best not to look at the satin curves I've bared. Not because I think it's wrong, but because, with my emotions oscillating wildly between relief, rage, and fear, I'm not sure I'd be able to stop myself from doing more than simply touching her.

Despite everything—or maybe *because* of everything—I want her so much I feel it in the very marrow of my bones. I ache to clasp her to me and bury myself in her, to forget that I've come so disastrously close to losing her—that I might still lose her if we don't win the battle with her cancer.

Tomorrow at noon, they will cut her head open to excise the tumor from her brain, and I'm fucking terrified.

Dragging in an unsteady breath, I take the remnants of the dress to the living room, where I chuck it into the fireplace to destroy the evidence of Alina's successful self-defense. Not that anyone will link her to the dead man—Valery's forensic team will get rid of the body and destroy all evidence of what occurred in that hostel room—but still, we can't be too cautious here, where we have much less influence with the police than we do back home. I'm relieved that nobody at the clinic commented on the blood stains. They most likely thought that the blood was from the gash in her hand. Or the miscarriage/period—whatever the bleeding at the end of a chemical pregnancy is called.

My chest squeezes painfully, a sensation that I ascribe to prolonged sleep deprivation. It's good that things turned out this way—the best possible outcome, really. Now Alina won't hate me for forcing her to proceed with the treatment that would've killed what she thought of as our baby girl. And even if it weren't for the necessity of the treatment, I don't know if I could've handled my Alinyonok being pregnant and giving birth—not after the nightmare about my mother's death.

I was so fucking wrong to try to force this on her, to think that tying her to me was worth inflicting this kind of physical trauma on her.

Well, never again. I'll have to win her love some other way.

And if I can't, I will keep her regardless.

I stay by the fireplace long enough to make sure the dress is nothing but ashes. Then I call Valery and confirm that his forensic team cleaned up the scene. The entire time, my eyes burn as if pepper-sprayed as I think of the tiny embryo that never was and remember the look on Alina's face when she told me she was bleeding.

I tell myself that they burn from fireplace smoke and from lack of sleep, not anything as banal as grief. There was nothing to grieve, after all. The baby never truly existed.

It's not until I return to bed and pull my sleeping wife against me that I feel a strange wetness underneath my eyes and realize the painful tightness never left my chest. Even now, as I'm holding what's most precious to me in the whole world, each breath feels like a struggle, each heartbeat requiring monumental effort.

Despite my exhaustion, hours pass before I'm able to finally fall asleep.

CHAPTER 11

ALINA

Valery and Konstantin are waiting in the reception area when Alexei and I walk into the clinic at half past eleven.

I stop in my tracks.

I don't know what I expected, but encountering my brothers calmly sitting here wasn't it. Alexei had to know they were here, and he allowed it. Does that mean—

"Hey." Valery is already crossing the room toward us, with Konstantin on his heels. "How are you doing?"

"I'm okay," I say warily, darting a glance at Alexei's face.

My husband's eyes are narrowed and his jaw is tight, but he's not reaching for any weapons, which I take as a good sign.

"We'd like to speak to our sister alone," Konstantin says, addressing him. As usual, my oldest brother lacks all subtlety—not that the situation requires any.

We all know where we stand.

"You can speak to her here and now, with me, or not at all." Alexei's lips stretch into a grim smile. "Your choice."

"It's fine," I say as Konstantin's nostrils flare dangerously. "We'll just take a few steps this way, okay? We'll be within your sight at all times."

Before Alexei can reply, I grab Konstantin's hand and drag him toward the reception desk, which is empty today. Valery immediately joins us, standing in such a way that the sprawling leaves of the six-foot-tall cane block most of his face.

I make sure Alexei isn't about to explode—he's glaring at us darkly but staying put—before I turn to my brothers. "Thank you both for coming. You didn't have to, but—"

"Nikolai and Chloe are on their way," Valery says in a low voice. "They'll be here tomorrow afternoon."

I can't hide a shocked gasp. "Really? With Slava?"

"No," Konstantin says in a similarly quiet voice. "They left him in the compound with Pavel. It's too dangerous for him here. Listen…" He leans in so his face is also blocked by the cane, and his voice drops to a barely audible whisper. "We're working on a plan to get you out. We can't do it before the surgery, but—"

"No." The word escapes my lips before I can consciously formulate the thought. "Don't."

Valery cocks his head. "Why?"

"I don't want anyone to get hurt."

I don't want my brothers to rescue me for the same

reason I didn't contact them when I escaped—because I don't want to endanger them.

And because the thought of being separated from Alexei again makes me feel like I can't breathe.

The realization is like a thunderclap in the middle of a clear sky, as disturbing as it is startling. But it's true. I don't want to be away from Alexei. Maybe it's the tumor messing with my brain, or maybe it's everything that happened yesterday and Alexei's irrational determination to take care of me no matter what, but the thought of being without him, of facing the battle ahead without his strength and resolve... I can't even imagine it.

I don't want to imagine it.

"Has he hurt *you*?" Valery asks, very softly.

I shake my head. "And he won't. But he will hurt the two of you. And Nikolai and Chloe. Please..." I shift my gaze from Valery to Konstantin and back. "Listen to me... I'm fine. I want to stay with him. Please don't do anything—not now at least."

Valery and Konstantin exchange a look.

"I mean it."

"She means it." Alexei's sardonic drawl makes me jump. Somehow, he's approached us without my noticing. His eyes gleam mockingly as he loops his arm around my waist to pull me to his side. "Now if you're done plotting against me, your sister has major surgery in a few minutes."

Valery reaches out and squeezes my hand. His

expression is the closest to strained I've ever seen. "Good luck. You'll do great."

"She doesn't need luck. She has the best doctors," Konstantin says. Adjusting his glasses, he gives me a level look. "You have a good chance of surviving this unscathed. According to one recent study, only one-point-seven percent of patients undergoing awake craniotomy had any sort of permanent side effects."

Alexei glares at him, but I just laugh. Because that's Konstantin for you—logical, factual, and lacking in anything resembling social niceties. He says what he thinks. In that, he's the polar opposite of Valery, whom one can never take at face value.

"I'll be okay, you guys," I say when I stop laughing. "See you in a few."

They nod, stepping back, and Alexei leads me through the reception doors into the hallway and to the room where the surgical team is already waiting for us.

———

As soon as we enter, the nurses have me change into a hospital gown, and then Fasseau informs me that they'll need to shave off a portion of my hair in order to perform the craniotomy.

"It won't be as much as usual," he says in a reassuring tone. "Our team tries to spare most of the hair by removing just a few strands around the incision and thoroughly washing the scalp to prevent infection. We understand that for women with long hair like yours, it can be—"

"Won't I lose it anyway with chemo?"

Fasseau looks uncomfortable. "Yes, most likely, but—"

"Then just shave it all off. I want to get it over with."

I don't look at Alexei as I say this. I don't want to see his reaction. If, despite all of his insistence to the contrary, he finds me repulsive with a bald head, it's better if he walks away now, before I grow even more reliant on him.

Before I lose sight of how it all began and why we shouldn't be together.

Fasseau shoots a helpless look at Ingels and the rest of his colleagues before turning his attention back to me. "Mrs. Leonov, are you sure about this? There's a chance, albeit a small one, that chemo won't be required—"

"Do as she says." Alexei's tone is harsh, but when he clasps my hand in his, his grip is extraordinarily gentle, as if he's afraid I'll break. "Shave it all off. Now."

Fasseau pales. "As you wish." He motions to the nurses, then pauses and turns to me. "Mrs. Leonov… you have such beautiful hair. Would you perhaps like to have a wig made of it?"

"No." My answer is unequivocal. For some reason, the idea of wearing my own hair as a wig is giving me the willies. "Just get rid of it, please. Or… give it to someone."

Fasseau's eyes brighten. "Are you sure? If you're

certain you wouldn't mind, we'd love to use your hair to make a wig for one of our pediatric patients. Her hair was almost exactly the same color and length as yours before she lost it, and she's been devastated about it."

I swallow the lump that forms in my throat. "Of course I don't mind. Please go ahead."

Just the idea of a child going through this… If I can lessen her pain in some small way, it's worth losing my hair a thousand times over.

A minute later, I'm seated in front of a mirror in the attached bathroom as one of the nurses shaves my hair with buzzing clippers, being careful to collect the falling strands into a bag as Alexei watches from the corner behind her.

She's extremely methodical about it, doing her best to preserve nearly all of the length, and for some reason, the experience is not nearly as traumatic as I imagined. Maybe it's because I know this will brighten a child's day, or maybe because, after everything, I simply can't bring myself to care about something as shallow as my appearance.

It's odd, but something inside me appears to have shifted. I don't know if it's the man I killed or the baby I lost, but I no longer feel like myself.

"All done," the nurse says cheerfully, and I blink, realizing I zoned out.

Though I've been facing the mirror the entire time, I somehow forgot to look at my reflection. So I look now—and I don't entirely hate what I see.

Bemused, I raise my hand and touch the fuzzy stubble covering my skull.

It feels... pleasantly prickly.

And tickly.

Also, my head is a bit cold.

My eyes meet Alexei's in the mirror. His gaze is demon dark and intense. And... filled with heat?

I blink, certain I've misconstrued his expression.

But no. The way he's staring at me is raising the temperature in the small bathroom by about a thousand degrees.

I flush, no longer the least bit cold as he steps up to me from the back, forcing the nurse to step aside. Lifting his hand, he runs it over my shaved skull, the warmth of his big, callused palm perversely making me shiver.

His voice is a soft, raspy rumble as he bends down to murmur into my ear, "I fucking love it."

The nurse clears her throat uncomfortably.

Ignoring her, he straightens and pulls me to my feet to face him. Clasping my face between his palms, he bends his head and slants his lips over mine in a raw, animalistic kiss that leaves me wet and trembling—and desperately wishing we were elsewhere.

"Um... excuse me..." The nurse's voice is high and more than a little squeaky. "We have to prep Mrs. Leonov for surgery now."

Alexei reluctantly straightens, ending the kiss, but his hands remain on my face, his gaze dark and scorching... and deeply worried.

I see the concern behind the heat, the fear that he can't quite mask, and for some reason, it makes me calmer. More resolved.

"It'll be all right," I whisper, laying my hands over his, and then I pull away to face the nurse. "I'm ready. Let's do this."

CHAPTER 12

ALEXEI

The next several hours are the longest of my life.

I insisted on being in the operating room, so just like the doctors and the nurses, I'm wearing a surgical gown, mask, gloves, and booties—and even so, I'm not allowed to get within three meters of my wife or to interact with her under any circumstances.

"If you startle us, the scalpel could slip," Ingels warned ominously. "You need to stay absolutely still and quiet at all times, or better yet, wait outside."

I promised to be still and quiet, and that's what I'm doing now: sitting in the corner like a ghost and staring intently as the team puts Alina under a combination of local and mild general anesthesia before hooking her up to a million monitors and strapping her head in place—I assume to prevent her from moving it once she's awake. The rest of her body is covered with surgical drapes, leaving only her head exposed, and then a portion of her skull is marked for an incision.

Stomach churning and chest tight, I watch as they use a drill-like instrument to create a bone flap and expose the grayish-pink tissue underneath.

Alina's brain.

Fuck.

I realize my hands are shaking, so I ball them into fists.

I've seen naked brains before, both blown out and intact. But this is different. It's not some enemy of mine. This is my *wife* lying there on the operating table, under the merciless glare of the bright surgical lights.

I know she's not feeling any pain and that this is necessary to save her life, but it doesn't make it any easier. I still want to go over there and crack open the skull of every person who's doing this to her.

Taking deep breaths, I squeeze my eyes shut, then force them open as Fasseau barks out, "Saline!"

The nurses are already on it, the entire seven-person team operating like a smoothly oiled machine. In addition to Ingels and Fasseau, the two neurosurgeons, there is an anesthesiologist, three nurses, and a neuropsychologist, all of them moving in a carefully orchestrated way.

And then... Alina is awake. Her long lashes flutter open, revealing her gorgeous jade-green eyes, and her tongue flicks out to moisten her plush lips. She blinks, once, twice, three times as the doctors start speaking to her, assuring her that everything's all right, reminding her of what's happening and where she is, asking if she's feeling any pain or discomfort. And... she answers.

She fucking answers them, as if she's not lying there with her brain exposed.

It's surreal to watch.

I understand now why Ingels explicitly warned me to stay still and quiet. The urge to come up and speak to her, to make sure she's all right, is overwhelming. Though she's just told the doctors she's not in any pain, I want to ask her that myself, to make sure she's not freaked out by what's happening to her—because I fucking am.

Still and quiet, I remind myself. Stay still and quiet.

So I do. I'm a human statue in the corner as the surgeons begin cutting into the exposed tissue, speaking to her the entire time. They make her count to a hundred and do multiplication tables. They ask her to sing and to speak in both English and Russian—and then translate from one language to the other and back. They remove some of the drapes covering her body and make her move her fingers and toes, then bend her arms and legs. They apply electric stimulation to various parts of her exposed brain and ask her what she sees and hears, if she feels any tingling when they do this and that.

It's the weirdest, most sci-fi experience of my life, and I'm not the one it's being done to.

I don't know how long the operation lasts, but my legs have fallen asleep by the time they put Alina under again and close up her skull, securing the bone flap with small titanium plates before suturing her scalp closed layer by layer.

I wait until they're completely done before I finally move, carefully standing up as pins and needles cut agonizingly through my legs. It takes a solid minute to regain most of the feeling in my feet, and by then, the nurses are wheeling Alina to the recovery room.

I hurry to accompany them there and then wait impatiently next to Alina until Ingels and Fasseau show up sans their surgical gowns and gear.

"Well?" I demand. "How did it go?"

"About as well as we could've hoped," Fasseau says, wearily rubbing a hand over his face. "There were no complications during the procedure, and we removed all of the tumor cells that could be removed without impacting healthy brain tissue—which, luckily, was nearly all of them. Now we're waiting on the pathology report to determine the exact tumor type and grade. That's what will tell us how aggressive the follow-up treatment will need to be."

I exhale a breath I had been holding. "And how long will this report take?"

"Normally, at least several days," Ingels replies. "But since your case is of the highest priority, our neuropathologist will work through the night, and we'll have the answers by morning."

They'd fucking better, given the high-seven-figure "donation" I've made to the clinic on top of their already-exorbitant fees.

I look at Alina, who's still sedated, her head thickly bandaged, and my chest tightens again. "When will she awaken?"

"Within the next twenty minutes or so," Fasseau says. "Our anesthesiologist used slightly stronger sedation at the end, just in case there were any complications as we were wrapping up. Luckily, there weren't."

Luckily indeed. If anything had gone wrong, he and his colleagues wouldn't have walked away alive.

I find Alina's limp hand under the blanket and squeeze it gently. Her long fingers are so thin, so fragile in my hold.

The need to protect her, to keep her from all pain and hurt, is overwhelming, and the knowledge that I can't is like a festering boil inside me. Watching her on that operating table today, being forced to stay still and silent as they drilled into her skull... I'm still not sure how I survived that. Or how I will be able to bear watching her suffer through the chemo and radiation.

But I will. Because she needs me, even if she doesn't want to admit it.

Although... maybe she did sort of admit it this morning. I overheard only portions of her conversation with her brothers, but it was obvious that they wanted to take her away and she refused.

It's possible she's just trying to avoid bloodshed, but I'm hopeful that it's more than that. That she's beginning to see what I've always known: that we belong together.

The doctors leave, and I carefully perch on the edge

of the bed and bring her hand to my lips, brushing a kiss over her knuckles. As I do so, I notice that the red polish on her nails is chipped—the first time I'm seeing her nails less than perfect in recent years.

Strangely, I like it. More than like it—I prefer it. Just like I prefer the way her face looks without any makeup, her porcelain skin baby soft, her lips naturally full and rosy, slightly parted to reveal that adorable tiny gap between her teeth. Even the heavy bandage on her head doesn't take away from the stunning symmetry of her features, the delicate beauty of which is only enhanced by the super-short buzzcut they gave her.

It was all I could do to stop with a kiss in that bathroom.

Fuck, even now I want her.

I take a deep breath and remind myself that she's sick, and that it'll be a long time before she recovers enough to handle the raw need pulsing through my veins and stiffening my cock.

No matter how much I crave her, I will restrain myself for the foreseeable future.

I'd never want to hurt her in any way.

CHAPTER 13

ALINA

I wake up with a headache, which is normal for me these days. Except… my head is sore too. On the outside.

Confused, I bring my hand to my head, and as my fingers brush over the thick bandage on my skull, the memories rush in.

Bright lights blinding me.

People in surgical gowns and masks hovering over me, telling me to do this and say that.

No pain but a terrifying awareness that they're cutting into my head as they bend over me with their surgical instruments.

Holy fuck. I survived an awake brain surgery.

It's done, and I'm alive.

And… feeling largely like myself.

I open my eyes to see Alexei bending over me.

His dark gaze is intensely concerned. "How are you

doing?" he asks, tenderly stroking my arm. "Are you in any pain?"

I moisten my dry lips. "Not really. Just a little sore. Could I... have some water?"

He's already handing me a cup with a straw.

I greedily suck down a few sips. "So how did it go? Did they get it all?" I know that's unlikely, but what if—

"We're still waiting for the pathology results," he informs me, taking back the cup I hand to him. "Hopefully, we'll have them by—"

The door opens, and Ingels walks in. "You're awake. Good." He approaches the monitors and checks everything, then takes my vitals before saying, "Everything's looking good. How are you feeling?"

"Surprisingly okay," I tell him, and he smiles widely.

"That's our goal. As the sedation wears off, you may feel some soreness and discomfort, along with continued headaches. That's absolutely normal and expected. If it gets to be too much, you can press this button"—he hands me a remote-like device attached to a small screen with lots of buttons—"and the PCA pump will dispense more pain medication. And, of course, don't hesitate to let us know if anything is bothering you. Our team will do whatever we can to make you comfortable."

I happen to glance at Alexei in that moment and catch him frowning at the device.

For a second, I'm confused, but then it dawns on me.

Is he afraid I'll abuse this like I've done with pain pills in the past?

On impulse, I touch his hand to get his attention. "I won't," I say quietly in Russian when his eyes meet mine. "I won't even push the button. You don't have to worry."

For some reason, despite the difficult road ahead, I don't feel the same need to escape reality as I did in the past. I don't know why that is, and I'm not ready to delve too deeply into it.

Alexei's stare is piercing, even as his reply is soft. "Okay. I trust you."

My breath escapes in a soft exhale, and I look away, not wanting to acknowledge how his words make me feel.

I trust you.

Why does he? He shouldn't. We're still enemies, or at the very least adversaries in this relationship he's forced us into. But he said he trusts me, and for some reason, I believe him. Does that mean I trust *him*? The man who puppet-mastered his way into my life using both violence and guile?

Once again, I don't know, and I don't want to think about it. The headache that I woke up with is getting worse, and I'm starting to feel mildly nauseated.

I close my eyes to combat the sensation, and when I open them next, my brothers are standing over me, with Alexei behind them, and it's getting dark out.

I must've drifted off without realizing it.

"Hey," Valery says softly. "You're awake. How are you feeling?"

He's speaking slowly, as if I've lost the ability to understand language. Which, I suppose, I could've. I mean, they cut into my freaking *brain*.

I don't know what prompts me to do it, but I make my face go slack and emit a zombie moan before growling in a mixture of Russian and English, "Brains, *mozghee*, brains…"

Valery sucks in a sharp breath, his face going a shade paler as he exchanges an alarmed look with Konstantin, but Alexei lets out a crack of laughter.

I grin, glad at least someone got the joke.

"Are you messing with us?" Valery asks incredulously, looking back at me, and I nod, laughing.

"Sorry. The opportunity was too good to miss."

Konstantin cocks his head. "It was, wasn't it? I take it you're feeling okay."

"I am. Definitely." And it's true. The headache is better, and I'm no longer nauseated. I'm also feeling a bit… euphoric.

Shit. Did they pump something into my IV while I was out? If so, I'll have to tell them not to. I promised Alexei I wouldn't abuse the pain meds, and I don't want the doctors to make a liar out of me.

I'm not sure why it matters to me so much, that I don't betray Alexei's trust in this, but I gave my word and I intend to honor it… even if the way I'm currently feeling is nice. So nice that—

"That's it. You've seen for yourself that she's fine,

and now she needs to rest," Alexei says, no longer laughing, and I blink, realizing I've closed my eyes again. "You can visit again tomorrow, and I'll send you an update as soon as we get the pathology results back."

I'm about to object, but he's already herding my brothers out of the room, so I let my lids drift shut and enjoy the pleasant sensation of only a mild headache and no nausea.

A low murmur of voices and some beeping pulls me out of another inadvertent nap.

I open my eyes and see that it's still dark.

A nurse is in the room, speaking quietly with Alexei as she checks my vitals. Noticing that I'm awake, she asks me a few questions, including such basics as my name, the current year, and who the president of Russia is. I'm tempted to pull the zombie routine on her, but I don't. Instead, once I answer the questions to her satisfaction, I tell her, "No more pain meds," and then I reiterate it as she fiddles with my IVs.

"Alinyonok…" Alexei's voice is gruff as he steps up to me. "You don't need to—"

"I do. I want to see how I really feel."

As I speak, I notice the dark circles under his eyes and the thick stubble on his jaw. Has he been at my side this whole time? I look past him and spot another bed in the room, a hospital gurney with unmade sheets that they must've recently wheeled in here.

My chest squeezes. He *has* been here this whole time. Why? He could've gone to sleep at his nearby penthouse, in his luxurious, king-sized bed. He knows

I'm getting the best medical care money can buy, and if anything had gone wrong during the night, he would've been only minutes away. But he insisted on staying here, in my hospital room—just like he's been at my side at all times ever since this nightmare began.

At all times except when I ran away.

"All done," the nurse cheerfully announces and hurries out of the room, leaving us alone.

On impulse, I extend my hand to Alexei. When he takes it, I wrap my fingers around his palm and say, "You should go and get some rest. You look tired."

A shadow of a smile touches his lips as he perches on the edge of my bed and brings my hand to his mouth to brush another kiss over my knuckles. "It's sweet of you to worry about me, Alinyonok, but I'm fine."

"You don't look fine," I say. "You look like you haven't slept in a week."

He chuckles. "That sounds about right." Gently, he places my hand on the bed and says, "How about we make a deal? You sleep, and I'll sleep."

Here, he means. By my side.

I sigh and close my eyes, not wanting to dwell on what it all means.

Not wanting to question if I've been wrong about him this whole time.

———

I'M WOKEN UP TWICE MORE DURING THE NIGHT BY nurses checking on me, and each time, Alexei is there. Finally, it's morning, and Fasseu comes in, a printout in his hands.

Without preliminaries, he announces, "We have the pathology results."

My heart leaps into my throat, and Alexei, who's sitting on my bed, visibly tenses.

"As my colleague, Dr. Kressler, suspected, it's a high-grade oligodendroglioma," the doctor continues. "However, there is some good news as well. The tumor has a characteristic that makes it more susceptible to radiation and chemotherapy—specifically, the codeletion of 1p/19q—which, combined with the frontal lobe location and your age, leads us to believe that a favorable outcome is more likely than not."

"So... better than a fifty-percent five-year survival rate?" I ask cautiously. Because that would be amazing. That would be—

"Maybe as high as eighty percent," the doctor says and smiles. "There's also an immunotherapy trial I'd like to enroll you into. We can do it in conjunction with the chemotherapy protocol, or prior to it—depending on your risk tolerance."

"Tell us more," Alexei orders, and the doctor launches into the explanation of the immunotherapy in question and how it harnesses the patient's own killer cells to fight the cancer. He goes over all the risks, many of them having to do with autoimmune reactions, and then he launches into the radiation protocol that I'd need to undergo regardless of whether I opt in for the trial or not. "It will be for six weeks, starting as soon as possible," he tells us.

I do my best to listen attentively and take it all in, but there's one question I can't stop dwelling on that the doctor isn't addressing. "What about freezing my eggs?" I ask as he pauses for breath. "Where does that fit in?"

The doctor glances warily at Alexei, who's watching him with narrowed eyes, before refocusing on me. "That is something for you two to discuss with a fertility specialist. We have achieved close to a complete resection—that is, the removal of all visible and detectable parts of the tumor—during the surgery, but some cancer cells inevitably remain, so there is always a risk to delaying the start of radiation therapy. However, given your age and the other favorable factors we discussed, it's not a big risk, and you have to decide how important the ability to have biological children is to you. Something to keep in mind is that the radiation therapy we'll be using is highly targeted and localized, so there will be no direct impact on your reproductive organs. There could, however, be an indirect impact on your fertility through changes in hormonal levels, as we may have to target areas near the pituitary gland and the hypothalamus."

"What about the immunotherapy?" Alexei asks, his dark eyes focused intently on the doctor.

"Since this specific drug is still in the clinical trial stages, we don't have a lot of data on how it impacts reproductive health. However, other immunotherapy drugs have been shown not to have a significant impact on reproductive organs, and we expect to see the same results here." The doctor pauses before adding, "Of course, if the immunotherapy is used in conjunction with the chemotherapy protocol, your fertility will almost certainly be affected. So it's really up to you and your risk tolerance..."

My head is beginning to ache again from all this doctor speak. I want straightforward answers about the path forward, not all this "your risk tolerance" hedging.

Alexei must feel the same because his tone sharpens as he asks, "So what do *you* recommend? Chemotherapy in conjunction with the immunotherapy and radiation? Or just immunotherapy and radiation?"

Fasseau takes in a breath. "Like I said, it really depends on—"

Alexei raises his hand, palm out, cutting him off. His tone sharpens further. "If this were your wife or daughter, what would you do for her?"

The doctor swallows, paling visibly, and I instantly feel bad for him. If he knows anything about Alexei— and I'm sure he does—he must suspect that it's not just his professional reputation on the line.

"I..." He takes another breath. "I would do the immunotherapy in combination with the radiation, with no delay. And I would hold off on the chemotherapy to see if those two protocols will suffice. Chemo is rough on the body and has all sorts of long-term side effects, including the possibility of other cancers, so if there's a chance you can avoid it…"

Alexei nods grimly. "Right." He glances at me, and his voice softens. "Alinyonok, do you have any other questions for the doctor?"

I feel like I have about a million, but none come to mind at this moment. The headache is worsening, and I just want some time to process all of this. "I'm good for now, thanks."

Fasseau nods and leaves the room. I wait until the door closes behind him before I reach out to touch Alexei's arm. "About the egg freezing…"

I don't know what I'm about to say. Do I want to delay starting the treatment and attempt to extract my eggs, despite what the doctor advised? And if they were to be successfully extracted, what then? Would Alexei insist on creating embryos with his sperm, thus permanently binding us together like he's always wanted?

Before everything that's happened, I would've fought that possibility tooth and nail, but now… I don't know what I want anymore. Or what I fear more: having children with Alexei or never being able to give him any.

His jaw tightens. "No."

I blink. "What do you mean, no?"

"You heard the doctor. We shouldn't delay the treatment."

"But shouldn't we speak to a fertility specialist first, so—"

He grips my hands, his gaze boring into me with fierce intensity. "I can't lose you."

"But—"

"No buts. The only thing we'll delay is the chemotherapy, for the reasons Fasseau outlined. The rest of it —the radiation and the immunotherapy—will start as soon as the doctors recommend."

I stare at him, equal parts confused and outraged. Wasn't he all about having a child with me before all of this happened? Has he changed his mind? More importantly, it's *my* health and fertility we're talking about, so don't I get to decide? Then again, this is the man who thought nothing of making me marry him and of impregnating me against my will—not to mention, arranging our betrothal when I was barely fifteen. I haven't forgotten any of this—how could I?—but somehow, my anger at him has faded in recent days, replaced by other emotions. Stupid, illogical, dangerous emotions like gratitude and... attachment.

No, not attachment. It's probably just a version of Stockholm syndrome. That's how it's supposed to work, isn't it? You humanize your captor, look for the good in him, become grateful for any kindness shown... And all the while, you're still at his mercy, fully in his power while you have none.

If there's anything I should be grateful for right now, it's that my husband is showing his true colors and reminding me why I've fought against this union— and why I must keep fighting.

With a jerky movement, I pull my hands out of his

grasp and demonstratively close my eyes. "I'm tired. I want to rest."

It's the coward's way out, I know, but it's the only escape he'll allow me.

Sure enough, his voice softens, the dangerous intensity in his tone fading. "Of course." He leans over me, and I feel the gentle brush of his lips over my cheek. "Sleep and get well."

I keep my eyes closed as he gets up, the bed dipping from his movement, and though by all rights, I should be too wound up to sleep, I find myself drifting off.

———

MY BROTHERS ARE THERE WHEN I WAKE UP AGAIN. AND not just Valery and Konstantin.

"Kolya," I exclaim as my middle brother comes up to stand over me, a faint smile on his lips. "When did you get here? Where's Chloe?"

At that moment, the door to my room opens, and Nikolai's wife steps in. I grin as her big brown eyes land on me, a bright smile illuminating her small, pretty face.

"Hey there! I hear you may have turned into a zombie," she says in American-accented English, and I laugh, glancing at Valery and Konstantin.

"You two sold me out, huh?"

A hint of amusement glimmers in Valery's normally impassive gaze. "Sorry to ruin your fun."

Like me, he's speaking English out of consideration

for Chloe. She's an American, and though she's learned a few Russian words and phrases since landing at Nikolai's Idaho compound, she's nowhere near being fluent in our language.

She makes her way over to me, and I carefully sit up, ignoring the jab of pain in my head as I extend my IV-free arm to hug her. Though I've only known Chloe for a few short months, I'm ridiculously happy to see her. Maybe it's because of the circumstances under which I left—carried away by Alexei after his brutal attack on the compound—but I feel like I'm reuniting with a sister instead of just a sister-in-law.

"How are you doing?" she asks, perching on the edge of the bed.

I'm about to reply when a flicker of movement catches my attention. I look across the room and meet Alexei's gaze. His expression is dark and forbidding as he stands in the corner, observing the scene, keeping an eye on me lest I vanish from under his nose again.

Seeing him brings back all the emotions from our most recent confrontation, and I force myself to refocus on Chloe. So what if he's watching us? I'm not plotting anything—at this moment, at least.

"You can see how I am," I reply to her, pointedly not looking in Alexei's direction. "Tell me, how is Slava?"

"He's good. Missing you," Nikolai says, coming to stand next to Chloe. He places his hand on her slim shoulder and moves his thumb over her nape in a massaging motion, as if he can't bear not to touch her. Which he probably can't.

My brother is beyond obsessed with his new wife.

"He wanted to come with us, but it wasn't a good idea," Chloe says, casting a wary look in Alexei's direction.

I can tell she wants to drill me about him, and if we were alone, that's exactly what she'd be doing right now. Alas, between my brothers and Alexei, we have zero privacy at the moment. Maybe I'll ask her to help me to the bathroom in a bit and fill her in. That is, if Alexei doesn't insist on accompanying me there instead.

For now, I keep the conversation focused on my nephew. "Is he making progress on his English?" I ask Chloe.

"Oh, definitely," she replies. "I've been reading lots of English books with him, and he's learned the names of all the animals. He's also working on his numbers and colors in English, and in general, I'm pretty sure he understands close to ninety percent of what I say."

"Good. I'm glad." I glance up at Nikolai with a smile. "He's becoming a little American. That's what you wanted for him, isn't it?"

My brother doesn't reply. He's busy shooting a murderous glare at Alexei, who's watching the room from the corner with the same dark intensity as before. Only now, his right hand is inside his black leather jacket, and Valery is mimicking his stance, while Konstantin is tapping out prime numbers with his foot, the way he often does when things get tense.

Shit. Did I miss something, or is this an inevitable consequence of too much testosterone in one room?

Whatever the answer, I need to diffuse the situation. Fast.

"Don't mind my husband," I say a little louder so Alexei can definitely hear me. "He's just being a bear because he's worried about me. Isn't that right, *Lyosha?*" I give Alexei a sugary smile as I use his brother's childhood nickname for him.

Alexei's gaze flickers toward me, and so does Nikolai's. Valery doesn't take his eyes off Alexei, but his hand leaves the inside of his jacket. A tense eyeblink later, Alexei drops his hand as well, and Konstantin stops tapping his foot.

I breathe out a sigh of relief. No idea what triggered the standoff, but cooler heads prevailed. Namely mine, which is literally cool where the bandage doesn't cover my shaved skull.

Speaking of which... "Do you like my new hairstyle?" I ask Chloe brightly, figuring it's best to just move on from whatever almost happened.

She cocks her head. "I do, actually. It's very Natalie Portman in *V for Vendetta*. I'm curious to see how it'll look without the bandage."

"Hopefully, you'll find out soon." I glance at Alexei. "Did they say when they'll take it off?"

"No, but I imagine it'll be in a couple of weeks," my husband replies, his tone cool and even as he eyes my brothers with unconcealed distrust.

"Will you still be here then?" I ask Nikolai. "How long are you guys visiting for?"

"Just a couple of days, unfortunately," he answers. "We don't want to leave Slava for too long."

"Totally understandable," I say. "I'm glad you guys came. Thank you for that."

"Of course," Chloe says and reaches over to squeeze my hand. "I'm so sorry this is happening to you. On top of… everything." Her gaze strays to Alexei for a brief moment, and I know the questions are eating her alive.

"Will you help me to the bathroom?" I ask, deciding not to put it off any longer.

"I'll do it," Alexei says, immediately stepping forward, but I lift my hand, palm out.

"Please, I'd rather a woman do it."

He narrows his eyes.

"I promise I'll call out for you if I need any extra help." He doesn't look convinced, so I add in a softer tone, "Please, Alexei… I need this."

Also, he knows the attached bathroom doesn't have any windows, but I don't point it out in case things get tense again.

His nostrils flare, but after a moment, he says, "I'll help you to the door, and she can go in with you."

Pushing past my brothers, he gently helps me off the bed and onto my feet. I'm still attached to an IV, so he maneuvers the metal stand to ride alongside me as he walks me to the bathroom door, keeping his arm looped around my back for support as Chloe trails after us. Thankfully, I'm minimally dizzy, so I can truthfully tell him that I'll be fine with only Chloe to help me.

As soon as we're inside the bathroom, Chloe closes the door and grabs my hand. "Oh my god," she whispers. "Alina, are you—"

"I'm okay. Truly." I keep my voice pitched low. "You saw it yourself: he's treating me well."

She gives me a dubious look.

"He is. And I know, it was a shock to me too. Look…" I squeeze her hand. "You and Nikolai had your differences in the beginning too. Some men can just be… intense." An understatement of the century when it comes to Alexei and Nikolai. "But it's worked out for you, and I'm hoping it will work out for me too."

She stares at me incredulously. "Are you saying you *want* to stay with him?"

"Yes," I lie.

Or at least I think it's a lie.

Either way, as much as I want to unload on her all the contradictory emotions tormenting me, I can't do so without putting her and Nikolai in danger. Right now, because of my illness, my brothers and Alexei appear to be in a fragile truce of sorts, a temporary ceasefire that could devolve into open warfare at the smallest provocation—and I'd like to extend this truce for as long as possible, even if we all know that my brothers will try to rescue me at some point, and that Alexei will fight them to the death before he lets them succeed.

Or… maybe he won't fight them that hard. Despite

his behavior thus far, there's still a part of me that's convinced he'll want to bail on this situation eventually.

Come to think of it, that could be why he's not worried about my ability to have children.

He no longer wants any with me.

The thought sears through me like a burn from a hot poker, and I must not hide it well because Chloe's expression grows concerned. "You're lying to me," she states in a low voice, and I'm forced to spend the next few minutes telling her all about how good Alexei has been to me in order to convince her otherwise.

I don't know if I succeed or not, but Alexei knocks on the door, and we're forced to end our private chat. Which is just as well because I'm suddenly very tired, and my headache is worsening. As soon as we emerge from the bathroom, Alexei helps me back to bed and ushers everyone out, claiming that I need to rest.

Which I do.

As I close my eyes, Alexei's fingers intertwine with mine, and I feel the warm brush of his lips over my cheek as I drift off.

CHAPTER 14

ALINA

On the doctors' advice, I start radiation and immunotherapy the very next morning, and my days become all about the various treatments. In between IVs and endless medical appointments, Valery and Konstantin visit as much as Alexei allows them, and so do Chloe and Nikolai before they return to the United States. I don't get a chance to talk to anyone in private again, but I think my family is somewhat reassured regardless because they can't *not* see just how dedicated Alexei is to me and to my recovery.

He's with me literally twenty-four seven. I don't know why he bothered with the penthouse nearby because he sleeps, eats, and works at the clinic. The uncomfortable hospital bed next to mine was swiftly upgraded to a luxurious extra-long king, and that's where Alexei sleeps—if he ever sleeps, that is. Whenever I wake up, he's always either watching me or working on his laptop, presumably keeping up with his business back home. Occasionally, Ruslan is there too, and I overhear them discussing various projects and investments, many of which I had no idea the Leonovs were into.

I've always thought my husband's family was more into shady, barely legal ventures, many of them involving weapons and the like. But cutting-edge pharmaceuticals and AI seem to be major interests of theirs as well, and they're big on philanthropy and supporting the arts. My husband has apparently made a major contribution to the new opera house that's being built in Moscow, and Ruslan is on the board of several charity organizations that oversee initiatives ranging from malaria vaccines in Africa to childhood literacy in disadvantaged areas of Central Asia.

Why aren't they better known for this stuff? I would think they'd want to shout about their charitable endeavors from the rooftops—anything to offset their terrible reputation. Unless... they like it that people think them cruel and ruthless.

I bet that kind of reputation could be an asset in certain business circles. Also, I wonder how much of said reputation is due to their father. Alexei is only thirty, and Ruslan is even younger, so it's possible that most, if not all, of the brutal deeds attributed to the Leonovs can be laid at the feet of one Boris Leonov.

Then again, maybe I'm just grasping at straws to justify my growing reliance on my husband and my increasing attachment to him. I hate to admit it, but I now crave his presence as much as I do his touch—and the latter not necessarily in a sexual way.

He's getting me addicted to him, dependent on him in much the same way that I'd once been dependent on the painkillers that helped my headaches. With him at my side, it's easy to keep my word and not abuse the meds I now have such easy access to. I don't need the meds because *he's* my pain relief, my stress reducer, my distraction from the anxiety that would otherwise consume me alive.

With Alexei, my illness is more than manageable.

At times, it's almost… pleasant.

My mornings start with a kiss and a gentle neck massage, followed by a breakfast of my favorite foods that he spoon-feeds to me, same as most of my meals. I don't know why I allow this, but I do—and for some reason, his feeding me helps me keep the food down despite the still-present nausea. On the one day I tried eating by myself like the grown-up I am, I threw up immediately, so I haven't tried again. Not only does his spoon-feeding me seem to be easier on my stomach, but the way he looks at me as he places each bite into my mouth makes me feel like my old self.

Wanted. Desired. Dangerously so.

My body may be battling a deadly disease, but it still responds to the dark heat in his eyes, to the scorching pull between us that nothing seems able to extinguish.

Not that he ever acts on that pull. He's careful with me nowadays, much too careful for my liking. It's as if he's afraid I'll break if he does anything more than give me a tender kiss. I won't break, but I don't know how to convince him of that—or if I should. After all, this is a marriage I didn't want, the culmination of a betrothal forced upon me when I was just a child. Except, with each day, it's getting harder to remember how it all began, to recall all the reasons why I shouldn't let myself fall for this man who takes such tender care of me.

Is it all an act? If so, for what purpose? We're already married. He has me where he's always wanted me—and yet nothing is as I imagined it would be.

I try to think back to my parents and their relationship, back before it took its darkest turn. Did my father ever take care of my mother when she was sick? I was a child, so maybe I didn't pay close attention, but I don't think he did. For all his toxic obsession with her, I can't recall a single instance when he so much as brought her a cup of tea while she was ill. In fact, I distinctly remember my mother being bedridden with pneumonia for a week when I was nine, and my father was entirely absent. I know that for a fact because I spent most of that week in my mother's room, so worried about her that I refused to go to school or play with my friends. My brothers spent a lot of time at her bedside too, but not my father.

Supposedly, he had a lot of work that week.

I hadn't given that incident a lot of thought—with the help of antibiotics, my mother recovered, and all was well—but now I can't help but to dwell on it... and to analyze every other aspect of their relationship.

In the past, all I'd seen were the parallels between my father and Alexei, but what stands out to me now are the differences.

Differences that I uncover more of every day.

"Do you ever drink?" I ask Alexei on an impulse one morning while we're waiting for the nurses to take me for a scan. "Like to the point of getting drunk?"

He considers it for a moment, then shakes his head. "Not really. As a teenager, I had too much vodka a couple of times, and I didn't like the feeling. I prefer to be clear-headed and fully in control, so if I do have any alcohol, it's usually a glass of wine or champagne with dinner."

"How very non-Russian of you," I say, half-jokingly, and he shrugs.

"That's what my father always said."

"Oh?" I'm extra intrigued now, as he hardly ever mentions the elder Leonov.

His expression undergoes a subtle hardening. "Yes, he's a fan of hard liquor. Vodka, cognac, whiskey. Ruslan likes that stuff too, but I don't."

It's strange how relieved I am. I didn't even realize I was concerned about it. "What about pot?" I ask, doing my best to keep a light tone. "Or… other substances?"

"Not my thing. I smoked a joint once when I was thirteen, but I didn't like how it made me feel, so I haven't tried anything stronger."

I stare at him, my relief battling with amazement… and more than a little embarrassment. Because I've tried a lot of stuff. Some more than once. Never enough to get truly addicted, but with my headaches providing a ready excuse, there were definitely times when I skated on the edge, when I stared into the abyss and knew that it would take only another pill or two to dive in and not emerge. And I wasn't always the one to step back from that edge. Sometimes, it was my brothers who pulled me back, forced me to stop when I might not have on my own.

How is it that Alexei is so much stronger than I am? He grew up with many of the same pressures, same temptations. In our circles, illegal drugs and expensive alcohol are offered at parties as frequently as hors d'oeuvres. One would have to be a saint to resist each time, and Alexei Leonov certainly doesn't qualify as that.

And yet… I can't deny that there's something perversely wholesome about my husband. Not soft. Not sweet. And definitely not good in the traditional sense of the word. But maybe… not entirely bad. Now that I've gotten to know Alexei better, it's easy to believe what Ruslan told me about their childhood, how Alexei took care of him and their sister more like a parent than an older brother.

It's easy to believe that because he takes care of me in much the same way.

As if I were precious.

As if I were truly his.

————

WEEKS PASS. ONE, TWO, THEN SOMEHOW THREE, FOUR, five, eight. Time moves both agonizingly slowly and disorientingly fast, the drag of never-ending treatments interspersed with days during which fatigue knocks me out like anesthesia. I feel like all I do is eat (and fight to keep the food down), sleep (and struggle to sleep), and undergo scans and treatments. And through it all, Alexei is there, comforting me, lending me his strength when I need it most.

Toward the end of treatment, he brings in Vika, and with the doctors' approval, she uses her needles to provide me with relief from the nausea and the headaches, so I start to feel better. Or maybe I'm feeling better because the combination of radiation and immunotherapy is actually working—something the doctors gleefully inform us of after yet another scan.

"I can't say that all the cancer cells are gone," Fasseau says with a big, beaming smile. "But they are not currently detectable on the highest-resolution images we have."

At my side, Alexei's ever-present tension seems to ease. "So the chemo—"

"Is not necessary at this time," Fasseau confirms.

My heart leaps sideways, then begins to beat in a new, oddly unsettled rhythm as I stare at the doctor, unable to utter a word through the growing tightness in my throat. The rational part of me understands and believes what the doctor is saying, but there's something deeply irrational inside me as well, something that doesn't dare to embrace so much as a sliver of hope.

"So she's in remission?" Alexei's voice sounds strange as well. Rough and almost... choked.

When I slant a glance at him, his onyx eyes are glittering with excessive brightness. I swallow and look away, not ready to think about what it means. Instead, I return my attention to the doctor as he answers in an upbeat tone, "It appears to be that way. There are also no markers of inflammation to suggest an autoimmune response to the treatment."

More good news. And I... don't feel right about it.

Not happy like I should be.

Not even relieved.

Instead, a heavy pressure is building behind my eyes, and the squeezing tightness descends from my throat into my chest.

I take a breath to combat the suffocating sensation, but my lungs don't seem to work correctly. So I try again, dragging in whatever air I can. But there's not enough air. Not even close to enough. My ears ring, my vision blurring as if I were underwater, and I grab Alexei's hand in panic, squeezing it with all my might.

Instantly, his gaze flashes to mine, full of undisguised concern, and as I look into those dark orbs, the suffocating tightness releases its hold on me, letting oxygen rush into my starved lungs.

Only then do I realize that my vision has blurred because of tears.

I'm crying, and the tears are not happy ones.

Nor are they sad ones.

I can't make sense of the way I'm feeling.

All I know is that Alexei wraps his strong arms around me and presses me so tightly against his chest that his heartbeat is a violent thunderstorm in my ear, his breath ragged gusts of wind on the top of my shorn skull.

Whatever my husband is feeling, I doubt it's as simple and straightforward as relief either.

Distantly, I'm aware of the doctor clearing his throat once, twice. When I reluctantly pull away from Alexei and give Fasseau my attention, his expression is somber again. And oddly sympathetic.

"If I might make a suggestion," he says gently. "You've been through a lot, Mrs. Leonov. With a diagnosis like yours, therapy is often highly beneficial." He glances cautiously at Alexei before adding, "Possibly for the both of you."

Therapy. I'd tried that once, and—I steal a look at Alexei, whose face might as well be carved from stone —it didn't exactly go well. But everything was different then.

I was different.

I don't know this new person who looks at me from the mirror, irrationally proud of the stubble on her head. Nor do I understand why, where there should be relief, there's only a growing sense of impending doom, a dread so deep that no amount of good news can obliterate it.

Maybe something went wrong during the surgery, and they cut off some crucial portion of my brain.

Or maybe therapy *is* a good idea.

"We'll look into it," Alexei says in a clipped tone, and I wonder if he means it.

Does he really want me dissecting our complicated relationship with a total stranger?

"So what are the next steps?" Alexei asks before I can do so. "Is Alina done with treatment?"

"With the active portion of it, yes." Fasseau shifts his gaze to me. "We'll continue to monitor you closely, Mrs. Leonov, but there's no longer any need for you to reside at the clinic, as long as you're able to come in for important scans."

"That won't be a problem," Alexei says. "Just let us know when, and we'll be here."

The doctor beams again. "Sounds good. Congratulations to you both."

With that, he departs, leaving us alone to process the news he's delivered.

Alexei grips my arm and turns me to face him. His face is taut, his eyes glittering once more. "Fuck, Alinyonok. You did it. You beat this thing."

Did I? It doesn't feel like it. But I nod anyway because that's what the doctor said. I have no reason not to believe him, especially since I *am* feeling better. Stronger.

Physically, at least.

Alexei pulls me into another long, fierce hug. Before I

can recover my breath, he cradles my face in his palms and, for the first time in weeks, kisses me with such unabashed hunger that I forget I've ever been ill. My entire body ignites, each cell coming back to life with a furious need that heats my skin and sends my heart racing. Panting, I cling to him, gripping his shirt in my fists as he bends me over his arm, devouring my mouth with a ravenousness that leaves no doubt of his intentions.

Finally, after treating me like a priceless glass figurine for so long, he'll fuck me hard, and I will enjoy every bit of it.

I'm honest enough with myself to admit that.

Except... he doesn't fuck me. Hard or otherwise. Breathing raggedly, he ends the kiss and, holding my hips to steady me, steps back. Then he releases me and takes another step back, putting more distance between us.

I stare at him as he shoves his fingers through his dark hair, agitated.

What the fuck just happened?

Did he not like kissing me?

"We should get you ready to go." His voice is strained as he drops his hand. "I'll make the arrangements with my security team."

And just like that, he's gone.

CHAPTER 15

ALINA

Within an hour, I'm hustled out of the clinic and across the street to Alexei's penthouse. Guards surround us as we make the short trip—way too many guards, and they don't even bother to stay out of sight.

What is Alexei afraid of? That I'll make a run for it the moment I'm out on the street? Or that my brothers will swoop in to snatch me away for good?

The latter is an actual possibility, to be fair. Though… if he doesn't want me anymore, shouldn't he be glad to be rid of me?

I steal a glance at his tense features as we ride the elevator up to the penthouse.

Does Alexei still want me? Could I have misread the way he pulled away after that kiss? We haven't had sex since before my escape, but I thought that was due to my state after the surgery and during the treatment. But maybe it was because he was starting to grow cold on me? Then again, if that were the case, why would he take care of me with such dedication? Out of some misguided sense of duty? Or is he feeling guilty for stalking me all those years?

Yeah, no, that doesn't sound like Alexei Leonov.

If he's taking care of me, it's because he wants to.

Which means he still wants me... right?

Dammit. Why do I even care? If the cancer treatment has made me undesirable to him, he'll just let me go, and all will be well.

Won't it?

"Here we are," Alexei says as the elevator doors open into the penthouse. "Are you hungry, or would you like to go straight to bed?"

"I'll take a shower first," I say.

And I'll thoroughly brush my teeth while I'm at it.

Maybe I smell like medicine, or worse.

"Wait," Alexei says, grabbing my hand as I start heading for the bathroom. "I'll come with you."

Oh.

My pulse speeds up.

His grip on my hand is firm and possessive. Very much my uncompromising captor.

Maybe I did misread his reaction to the kiss.

Maybe he just wanted to get me here, where we have more privacy.

I'm all but shaking with anticipation as he leads me to the bathroom, where he helps me undress, his eyes darkening to pitch black as the clothes come off my body. His touch isn't overtly sexual—his hands don't linger on my skin any longer than necessary as he helps me disrobe—but it's still electrifying, each brush of his fingers sending arrows of heat straight to my core until my knees are literally weak with need.

I want this.

I want what only he can give me—that dark, violent pleasure that both destroys and renews me.

I need it to feel whole again.

It's only when I'm completely naked that I realize he's still clothed—and making no moves to undress himself. Instead, he steps away from me and goes to turn on the shower, testing the water with his fingers as he adjusts the faucets to his satisfaction.

The heat inside me cools drastically.

Is he not joining me? Then why is he here?

"Go ahead," he says gruffly without looking at me. "Step in."

"Are you…" I hesitate, hating how insecure I feel. "Are you coming in too?"

His entire body tenses. "No." His voice is rough. "I'll take one later. I'm here to help in case you don't feel well."

So I didn't misread it earlier. He doesn't want to have sex with me. Even here, where we're not likely to get interrupted by any doctors or nurses.

I try to ignore the acidic tightness in my throat as I step under the warm spray and reach for the shampoo. One benefit of not wearing any makeup is that I don't have to worry about raccoon eyes as the water hits my face.

Or as tears mingle with said water, leaking from my eyes despite my best efforts to hold them back.

I don't even know why I'm crying again. This is fine. More than fine. So the man who forced me to marry him doesn't want me. That's a good thing. If this persists, he'll soon realize that whatever irrational obsession he developed when I was a teen has faded. At that point, he'll probably file for a divorce, and I'll be back with my family.

I'll finally be free.

I want to tell him to leave now, to let me be alone in the bathroom, but I'm afraid he'll hear the tears in my voice. So I just silently shampoo what little hair I have and scrub my body, soaping up three times to get rid of all traces of the clinic.

By the time I'm done, my tears have dried up, though I'm no calmer.

When I started treatment, I dreamed of this day, of being told that I'm in remission. I thought it would be the best day of my life. Instead, I'm a hot, weepy mess. And I don't think it's entirely because of Alexei's rejection, though that stings like a thousand riled-up wasps. It's everything combined, these strange, illogical emotions that are choking me like some carnivorous vine.

Inappropriate, inexplicable emotions like anger.

And guilt.

And resentment.

The deeper I dig, the more I realize that I'm fucking *furious* that this happened to me. The cancer, the miscarriage, *my parents' deaths*. And Alexei is smack in the middle of it all, his obsessive desire for me the only constant in the never-ending upheaval of my life, as much a relief valve for my turmoil as a contributor to it.

And now that constant is no longer there.

He doesn't want me anymore.

A burning knot swells in my throat again as I turn off the water with jerky movements. Alexei is already by the door of the stall, holding out a fluffy white towel, ready to wrap me in it as soon as I step out.

It's so nice of him. So fucking considerate.

It makes me want to rip his head off.

Who the fuck does he think he is, invading and manipulating my life all this time, marrying and impregnating me against my will, only to end up treating me this way? Like... like I'm his fucking *sibling* that he needs to parent.

Like all he feels for me now is pity.

Teeth clenched, I step out of the stall and duck to avoid the towel coming toward me. "I'll air dry," I say tightly. "Better for my skin that way."

And it's not like I have long hair dripping everywhere. Or that needs to be washed beyond a quick shampooing. A buzzcut is fucking amazing that way. I never knew what I was missing by having that long, heavy hair weighing me down all the time.

Frowning, Alexei steps back and hangs the unused towel. "Are you feeling okay?" His deep voice is laced with concern. "Any nausea or headache?"

Shockingly, no. Or maybe yes, but I'm too mad to notice. Instead of a reply, I march over to the sink, squirt out half a tube of toothpaste onto an electric toothbrush, and shove it into my mouth, using the loud buzzing to muffle the roaring anger inside me.

Anger that, deep down, I know he doesn't deserve. Not today. Not after the way he's been during my treatment. But I can't help it.

There's a caged beast inside me, and it's clawing to get free.

Frown deepening, Alexei comes up behind me as I spit out the glob of toothpaste burning my mouth with its extreme mintiness.

Our eyes meet in the mirror.

Like me, he's lost some weight in the past few weeks, and his sharply cut jaw and cheekbones look even more defined, his masculine features even more beautifully, cruelly chiseled. His dark eyes are slightly sunken, circled with shadows of lingering exhaustion. Even on the king-sized bed in the clinic, he didn't sleep well. Or eat well when he was awake.

I know all that, and guilt is a bitter-tasting foam on the bubbling rage inside me. I have no right to feel so angry when Alexei has been nothing but kind during these awful weeks. A model husband by any measure… if one ignores our history, of course.

"What's going on?" he asks, laying his hands on my shoulders and squeezing gently. Oh-so-fucking gently, like I'll break if he applies more pressure. "Is something wrong?"

"Nothing's wrong." I set the toothbrush on its charger with a sharp motion. "What could possibly be wrong?"

Other than the fact that I'm standing here buck naked and dripping wet in front of him, and he doesn't give a flying fuck. I might as well be a stick figure for all the sexual interest he's showing in me.

Keeping his touch maddeningly gentle, he turns me around to face him. His gaze is penetrating, deeply searching. "What is it, Alinyonok?"

Nothing. Everything. I want to scream that at him, but he'll think me insane. Fuck, I *feel* insane, completely out of control. I'm actually shaking from the effort it takes to contain the explosive emotions inside me.

I can't let them loose.

I don't know what will happen if I do.

"You can tell me," he urges softly. "I'm here for you. You know that."

"Are you?" The words burst out of me. Immediately, I want to take them back, but it's too late because more are coming on their heels. "Why would you be, when you don't want me anymore? When I'm now this"—I jerk out of his hold to gesture down at myself—"this sick, damaged *thing*?"

Even without a mirror, I can see my post-treatment body as he must: the protruding hipbones and knobby knees, the unmanicured toes and the fading rash on my calves from one of the medications. My breasts are smaller, my ass has all but disappeared, and my face hasn't seen makeup in so long I've forgotten what lipstick looks like.

And that's before I even think about the scars and the almost-buzzcut on my head.

Why on earth did I imagine he would want this version of me?

At my words, his eyebrows snap together. "What the fuck are you talking about?" His voice is low and dangerous. "You think I don't want you?" Face darkening, he advances on me, and I instinctively back away until my back presses against the glass wall of the shower stall as he continues through gritted teeth. "You think that all this time, I haven't been holding back with the greatest fucking effort?" His palms slap against the glass on either side of my head, pinning me in place. "That it hasn't taken every bit of my willpower to avoid taking what I want from this 'sick, damaged thing?'" He grinds his hips against my stomach, and I gasp as I feel the massive bulge in his jeans.

An erection that wouldn't be there if he didn't want me.

My heart pounds as I stare up at him. He looks... savage. Feral. His teeth are so tightly clenched a muscle pulses by his ear, and his mouth is a brutal slash above his too-sharp jawline. Even his hair, a couple of inches too long due to a missed haircut or two, seems to have given up on any pretense of civilization, tousled black locks falling haphazardly over his eyebrows and tempting my hand to brush them back.

My voice, when it emerges, is something between a squeak and a croak. "So… you are still attracted to me?"

Despite the incontrovertible evidence in his jeans, something pathetic in me still wants to hear him say it.

He leans down until only a few centimeters separate our faces and I can see the red striations in the whites of his eyes. "Attracted to you? I fucking *crave* you, Alinyonok. Sick or well, weak or strong, bedridden or dancing around, it doesn't matter. As wrong as it was, I wanted you eleven years ago, when you were still a child, and I want you today—only infinitely more. My obsession with you has no bounds, no parallels to anything. I want you when you're sleeping and when you're awake, when you're eating and when you're puking your guts out. I even wanted you when you were lying on that operating table with your head cut open, and if that's not fucked up, I don't know what is." Before I can draw in a shocked breath, he continues grimly. "I'm pretty sure I'll want you on your deathbed. And on mine. Every day, every hour, every moment of my existence is a never-ending battle for control around you, a battle that I'm fucking losing."

With that, he grips my face with his big hands and crushes his lips to mine.

CHAPTER 16

ALINA

I don't know what I expected, but the total collapse of Alexei's self-control wasn't it. He's shuddering with the force of his need as he devours my mouth, his jean-clad erection grinding against my stomach with rough, rolling motions, leaving no doubt of where his cock wants to be. And that's where I want it too, as deep inside me as it can go, taking me over that exquisite edge beyond which no fear, no rational thought can survive.

Beyond which there's only agony and ecstasy, a pleasure so incandescent it burns.

Panting, I wind my arms around his neck, matching his hunger with my own. Already, my entire body is alight with sensations, as if tiny fireworks are exploding underneath my skin. My nipples are hard and pebbled, aching for the suction of his lips, and I can feel the growing slickness between my legs, a tell-tale wetness that no longer embarrasses me.

I don't care if he knows how much I want him.

How much I've always wanted him, from the first day we met.

Tearing my lips away, I tell him that in a ragged whisper, and a low growl rumbles in his throat in response. Dipping his head, he grazes his teeth over the sensitive spot behind my ear, and I moan, my nails digging into the heavy muscles of his upper back as liquid heat surges down my body, adding to the desperate need coiling inside me, a pulsing tension that only he can relieve.

And he does. Wedging his hand between us, he parts my folds, his middle finger circling over my aching clit before pushing deep inside me. At the same time, the heel of his hand grinds against my sex, applying just the right pressure in a rhythm that heightens the tension to an unbearable degree, leaving me suspended on the sharpest edge of pleasure for a long, breathtaking moment before the sensation crests and the orgasm crashes into me like a wave breaking over the shore, the ecstasy simultaneously shattering and healing.

Breathing hard, I slump into his arms, but he's not done. Far from it. Gripping my ass, he hoists me up, forcing me to wrap my legs around his hips, and then I hear the metallic slide of his zipper and feel the thick, prodding pressure of his cock at my entrance.

Then he pauses, his chest heaving, and I dazedly open my eyes to meet his gaze.

His eyes are coal black, his forehead dappled with

sweat as he stares down at me, his jaw working from side to side. "I… won't be gentle." His words are strained. "I can't hold back today. If you need me to stop—"

I slam my lips over his, cutting off his noble offer. Or maybe it was a warning.

Either way, I don't want gentle from him. I didn't want it when he was my enemy, my stalker, my captor. And I don't want it now that he's my… whatever he is. I can't think of the right word as his tongue sweeps hungrily into my mouth and his long, thick cock penetrates me in one hard thrust, sending shockwaves through my nerve endings. Even as drenched as I am, it hurts, the stretch too much to bear after long weeks of abstinence, but there's a pleasure in that hurt, in that too-full feeling.

He's so deep inside me that we're one, fused together as much by flesh as we are by our shared past and our tumultuous present. And our future, whatever it may hold.

As he begins to move inside me, the savage power of his thrusts moving me up and down the glass behind me, winding me up until I reach another explosive peak, I find the word that I was looking for.

Everything.

He's now my *everything*… and I don't know how to wrap my mind around that.

Chapter 17

Alexei

I'm in both paradise and hell. Simultaneously, I'm burning alive and soaring above the clouds, the tight, wet clasp of Alina's flesh driving me past the point of no return. My mind is void of all but the most primal need, a lust so violent and all-consuming I can't think of anything but getting deeper into her, so deep she'll never be separate from me again, never doubt that she's anything but *mine*.

She comes again, crying out my name, her inner muscles clamping around my cock, and my balls draw tight, electric heat coursing up and down my spine as my own orgasm approaches. *No. Fuck, no.* I want this to last forever. *Need* it to last forever. But after weeks of nothing but my fist, my hunger is too overpowering, my self-control completely nonexistent.

With a groan, I surge into her one final time and explode, scorching ecstasy engulfing my senses as I empty myself within her silken depths, flooding her with my cum as aftershocks ripple through my body, one after another.

Slowly, my mind clears, and I open my eyes, realizing I'm still holding her pinned against the shower stall, my softening cock seated deep within her as I hold her up by her splayed thighs.

Thighs that I'm gripping way too hard, so hard she'll have bruises there tomorrow.

In general, I was rough. Much too rough given her fragile state.

Fuck. What have I done?

Our first time after her treatment should've been in a bed, with me carefully controlling every touch so as not to hurt her. The plan was to let her rest and get some sleep while I took the edge off with my fist, and then, once she was awake and rested, I'd wine and dine her before making love to her as if for the first time ever.

Instead, I lost control. Again. And there's no fucking excuse for it... even if she seemed to want it.

Worse yet, I didn't use a condom after I'd sworn to myself that I'd never endanger her health again.

Motherfucker.

I try to remember what her medical chart said about her last period—and relief floods my body as I realize she's due to start her period in a couple of days and is thus highly unlikely to be fertile.

Not that this negates my stupidity and lack of self-control.

Carefully, I pull out and lower her to her feet,

searching her face for signs of distress. "Alinyonok…" My voice is tight with self-loathing. "Did I hurt you?"

She blinks up at me, her jade eyes soft and hazy. "No… I mean, kind of, but in a good way."

Fuck. I knew it. I'm everything she's accused me of being: a selfish monster.

Like your father, a voice deep within whispers, but I shut it out.

Even on my worst day, I'm not like him.

I will never be like him.

But I *am* a fucking animal when it comes to my wife.

My fresh-out-of-cancer-treatment wife.

"Let's get cleaned up, and I'll let you rest," I say, mentally kicking myself as I guide her back into the shower, where I swiftly strip off my clothes and throw them on the mat outside the stall before turning on the water.

I wish it were cold water, but she doesn't deserve to be punished for the craving awakening in me again even as guilt eats me alive. So I make the water warm and ignore my growing erection. I will wash her as chastely as any nun—

"I don't want to rest," she says huskily when I face her, soap in hand.

And before I can say another word, she drops to her knees in front of me and takes my cock into her mouth.

CHAPTER 18

ALINA

I wake up sore, satisfied, and happier than I can recall being in years. Only a faint echo of a headache pulses behind my temples when I open my eyes and stretch, feeling like a well-fucked cat.

Or a woman who's been told she'll live, and whose husband demonstrated several times yesterday exactly how much he still wants her.

It's insane how much better I feel this morning. Maybe it's the orgasms, all five or six of them, or maybe I just slept better here than at the clinic, but the strange emotions of yesterday and my illogical response to the good news are muted, more of a memory than something that currently weighs on me. I can actually feel the joy and relief that I should've experienced when the doctor told me I'm in remission, even if a part of me is still afraid the cancer will return.

I don't know if that fear will ever go away, but I can live with it.

Because the treatment worked, and I'm going to *live*.

Grinning from ear to ear, I leap out of bed—only to wince at the pulling soreness deep inside.

Yeah, okay, there's a chance I may have over-done it yesterday. I mean, I all but forced Alexei to have sex with me again. And again. And again. Not that there was much force involved—all I needed to do was touch him, and he took over from there—but still, that's not something I ever imagined I'd do.

I'm still not ready to put a label on the way I feel about the man who'd manipulated my life for a decade and forced me into marriage, but it's no longer as simple as resentment and hate.

Maybe it never was.

I grab a robe and am about to head to the bathroom when my gaze falls upon a phone.

And a laptop.

Both are sitting pretty on the nightstand, right there within my reach.

What the hell?

Cautiously, I pick up the phone. It's the latest Samsung model, with a nice, big screen.

A screen that's locked, of course.

Only, as I stare at it, it unlocks itself.

"It's for you," Alexei's deep voice says, and I jump a foot into the air, nearly dropping the phone as my heartbeat leaps through the roof.

When the fuck did he come in?

I whirl around to see his tall, dark figure standing in the doorway, an inscrutable smile on his face.

Is this a trick? A test? "Um… thank you?"

"You're welcome." He comes deeper into the room. Unlike me, he's already dressed in a pair of jeans and a dark T-shirt that exposes the tattoos on his powerful arms. "Your brothers have been on my case to get you a phone of your own so they can get a hold of you whenever, but I didn't want them bothering you during treatment."

Or, more likely, until he decided I wouldn't coordinate an escape plan with them.

Is that what this is? A gesture of trust? Does he think I've accepted our marriage?

My heart picks up pace again.

Have I accepted it? Do I actually want to stay with him now?

"The laptop has the game you started on it," he continues before I can answer myself. "I've loaded our latest AI model on it, in case you'd like to use it to help you with the coding process."

I blink. Did I hear that right? "You're developing a proprietary AI?"

Alexei nods. "One of our companies is, yes."

Huh. Do my brothers know that? Probably. I bet Konstantin's team is already working on something similar or even more advanced.

"Thank you," I say sincerely. "Now that I'm feeling better, I'd love to resume working on the game." And with the help of AI, I may get very far, very fast.

"That's what I figured." He stops in front of me, his smile taking on a soft, sensual edge. "How are you feeling this morning, my beauty?"

My face heats at the memories of yesterday. "I'm... fine. Great, really."

He lifts his hand to run the edge of his callused thumb over my lips. "Your lips still look swollen." He brushes his fingers over my neck, sending a pleasurable shiver streaking down my arm as he gently presses on the sensitive spot under my ear. "And you have a hickey right here."

I flush hotter. My brothers will likely visit us today, and they'll see that. Unless... "Did you bring my makeup from the boat here, by any chance?"

Alexei nods. "It's in the bathroom, waiting for you." Eyes glittering, he adds, "Though I prefer you without any."

He does? That's... unexpected. "I need it for the hickey," I say breathlessly, taking a small step back.

The look on his face makes me think he's recalling yesterday in graphic detail, and as much as I'd love a repeat, I need to shower and brush my teeth first.

Alexei drops his hand and also takes a step back, curling his fingers into a fist as if to stop himself from reaching for me. "Makes sense." His voice is a touch hoarse. "Come to the kitchen when you're ready. Breakfast is waiting."

He walks out, and I exhale a breath I didn't realize I was holding.

Just that brief touch from him, and my body is

already thrumming with heady awareness, my pulse racing from being in his presence.

Or from the knowledge that I now have access to a phone.

Yes, that's what it is. I seize on the explanation because I'm not ready to analyze the complex, contradictory mess that is my relationship with Alexei. Instead, I lift the phone I'm still clutching in my hand and eagerly swipe across the screen.

Since I gave Alexei access to my cloud's login, I'm not surprised to find that this new device is filled with all my usual contacts and photos.

I'm not surprised, but I'm definitely excited.

I can call or message whomever I wish. Like my brothers. And Chloe. And my college friends. And Natasha back home.

Holy shit, I can even reach out to Birgit if I find her info.

I start by firing off a text to Konstantin and Valery to let them know I'm all right and have a phone. Then I do the same with Nikolai and Chloe.

My text to her has barely gone out when her video call request shows up, with Slava's little face—a copy of Nikolai's when he was a child—filling most of the screen.

My chest squeezes.

My nephew. I've missed him so much.

"Slavochka!" I grin so widely my ears hurt. "How are you?"

I'm speaking Russian, but the reply that comes my way in a high, pure child's voice is in English. "I'm fine."

I gasp and switch to English. "Wow, look who's become a little American!"

Chloe's face appears next to Slava's. "He's gotten so, so good at English," she says proudly. "We're actually starting to work on his Russian so he doesn't forget it, as he's developed a definite preference for English. Oh, and he's learning to read in both languages now."

I gasp again, more dramatically. "You're reading in both languages? Slava, that's amazing!"

My nephew puffs out his cheeks. "I can already do three-letter words. And bigger in Russian."

"Longer," Chloe corrects. "You can read *longer* words in Russian."

"Longer," Slava repeats obediently, and I marvel at how much he's changed and matured since Nikolai stole him from Boris Leonov and brought him to Idaho. Even in the couple of months since I've been gone, my nephew seems to have undergone a transformation, losing even more of his shyness and reticence, becoming more like a little adult.

"Where's Nikolai?" I ask Chloe as Slava disappears from view—likely off to play. "Or is it just the two of you hanging out this evening?"

"Nikolai is out with the guards, working on a few things." She doesn't expound on it, and I understand why. Ever since Alexei's attack on my brother's compound, Nikolai has been obsessed with beefing up their security. Chloe told me a little about his efforts when they visited, and I definitely approve.

The Leonovs should have no reason to attack Nikolai again, but the same thing can't be said for our other enemies. Of course, that first bit assumes I stay with my husband.

"So I heard the good news," Chloe says, a bright smile lighting up her pretty face. "You're in remission!"

"I am." I beam back. "They'll be monitoring me closely for a while, but no more treatments unless… you know."

"Right." She tilts her head. "Can you talk?"

We *are* talking, but that's not what she means.

"Alexei is not here," I say openly. "But I'm pretty sure this phone—and all my communications—will be monitored."

And I don't care if Alexei knows that I know that.

Chloe nods, unsurprised. "Just tell me then… What are you going to do now that you're out of treatment? Are you returning to Moscow or staying in Geneva for a bit?"

Good question. "I still need to discuss that with Alexei. He's actually waiting for me to have breakfast, so we'll catch up some more later, okay?"

"Okay. I'll tell Nikolai you called. He'll be very happy to hear you're doing well."

I blow her an air kiss and disconnect. Valery's call request is already on my screen, and one from Konstantin appears a second later. I decline them both, as my need for the bathroom is growing more urgent.

I'll talk to them as soon as I'm done with my morning routine.

————

WHEN I FINALLY ENTER THE KITCHEN AFTER HAVING reassured both Konstantin and Valery that I'm fine and don't need their help, Alexei is waiting for me, a big jar filled with a green smoothie in his hand.

"Drink this," he orders, handing it to me.

I sniff the contents of the jar. "What's in it?"

"Everything your body needs to recover. A dietician I consulted gave me the recipe, along with the rest of your meal plan."

"I have a meal plan?"

"You do." His dark eyes glint. "Now drink up."

Gingerly, I take a sip. It's not bad. A little sweet, more than a little grassy, and generally very healthy tasting. It's not what I would've chosen this morning, but since I'm not nauseated, I can stomach it.

My body probably does need the extra vitamins or whatever.

Alexei watches intently as I drain the jar, and then he makes me eat a piece of sprouted whole-grain toast with white-bean hummus—for the plant-based protein, he explains. Apparently, a whole-food plant-based diet is best for cancer prevention and remission maintenance, so that's what I will be eating going forward.

"Uh-huh." Why am I not surprised that it's a decree

and not a request? "And you're going to be eating all those plants alongside me?"

Alexei doesn't bat an eye. "If it helps you." He gestures to the sink, where I spot an empty jar and a small plate waiting to be washed. "I had the smoothie and the toast when I woke up. Wanted to make sure I got the recipes right for you."

I pause mid-bite. "You made all this yourself? From scratch?"

"Do you see anyone else in the kitchen?"

No, but… "I didn't know you could cook."

"I can follow directions." He pulls out his phone and swipes across the screen to show me the detailed recipes the dietitian sent him.

I set down my plate and scroll through them. The new diet will definitely be healthy. And possibly edible. The toast I'm eating is surprisingly good, the bread earthy and the hummus rich and creamy, but the jury is still out on the rest of the recipes, though I do see my favorite breakfast of *grechka* with berries on the list.

"I made sure the meal plan took your preferences into account," Alexei says when I look up from the screen. "I want you to be healthy *and* happy."

My heart skips a beat before launching into a gallop. The dark intensity in his gaze makes my skin burn even as his words wrap around my chest like barbed wire.

This is Alexei in a nutshell: obsessive, controlling, yet good to me in so many ways. The more time we spend together, the harder it becomes to remember that this is the same man who's killed dozens to force me into marriage. Or maybe it's not the remembering that's hard but the proper feelings associated with those recollections, the outrage and resentment that should be there but are increasingly difficult to generate.

I clear my throat and look away, picking up my plate to have something to do. "So what's the plan now?" I ask, demolishing the rest of the toast in a couple of bites. It really *is* tasty. "Are we going back to Russia or staying here for a while?"

"Your doctors have arranged ongoing monitoring for you in a specialty clinic in Moscow, so we're flying home tomorrow. We'll only need to return here for some key scans in a couple of months."

I set down my empty plate. "And where exactly is 'home?'"

From *my* stalking of him, I know Alexei divides his time between Moscow and St. Petersburg and has several residences in both. He also travels quite a bit for business.

Will he expect me to travel with him? Go to all the fundraisers and parties?

The idea is not nearly as unappealing as it should be.

"I had a house built for us just outside Moscow," Alexei replies. "So that's where we'll be heading when we leave here. If you don't like it, we can build something else at a location of your choosing."

"You mean I'm going to actually get a say in where

we live?" The question comes out snarkier than I intend.

His dark eyes narrow. "Of course. You're my wife, not my prisoner."

I can't help myself. "So long as I don't try to run, right?"

His jaw tightens, and he steps toward me. "Do you intend to run, Alinyonok?" His voice turns silky. "Are your brothers getting ready to stage a dramatic rescue?"

"You know full well they're not." Because I'm dead certain he listened in on my conversations with them, both via phone and in person.

He doesn't even bother to deny it. "Or so they want me to think."

For all I know, he may be right. But what I say is, "I'm not aware of any plan, and if I were, I'd dissuade them from it."

He closes the remaining distance between us to brush his knuckles over my jawline. As usual, his touch sends a wave of heat down my body, making my inner muscles tighten—an involuntary response that highlights just how sore I am.

"Because you don't want to leave me, or because you don't want them to get hurt?" he asks softly, his dark eyes boring into me. "You know I won't let them take you either way, right?"

I draw in an uneven breath. "I do know that."

This morning, at least. Yesterday, I wasn't so sure.

"So *do* you want to stay?" His eyes gleam, a

dangerous light entering their depths. "Or are you waiting for another opportunity to slip away?"

I fight the urge to avert my eyes again. "Does it matter? If you're going to keep me either way?"

He cups my jaw in his big palm. His voice softens, as does the black gaze holding me captive. "What do you think, Alinyonok?"

It does matter to him. I can see it on his face. Just like it mattered to me yesterday whether he still wanted me. This may have started off as an unhealthy obsession on his part, but it's grown into something more for him... just as it has for me.

I can no longer deny it. Not to myself and not to him.

"I..." My heart thuds as I reach deep for my courage. "I do want to stay."

That's all I can tell him right now, but it's enough. His eyes flare with dark heat, and even before his lips crash into mine and dishes on the table go flying, I know I've just sealed my fate.

If there was ever hope he would let me go, it's gone now, burned to ash by the ferocious need that consumes us both.

Demolished by the fate that chained us together long ago.

CHAPTER 19

ALEXEI

By the time I've cleaned up the wreckage in the kitchen, Alina is asleep on the couch in the living room, curled up under a throw in comfortable-looking sweats. Her open laptop sits on the floor next to her.

She must've started working on the game before exhaustion caught up with her. My Alinyonok is still far from regaining her full strength.

Quietly, I approach and stop next to her, self-loathing battling with primal satisfaction as I take in her kiss-swollen lips and the fresh whisker burns marring her porcelain skin alongside yesterday's hickey. In repose, her beauty is angelic, so pure it hurts, and the signs of my defilement of her are as much of a perverse turn-on as they are a cause of regret.

She's mine. All mine.

She admitted it. Told me she wants to stay.

And I, like the fucking animal I am, lost control and took her again.

Right there on the kitchen counter.

My only consolation is that I was gentle afterward. In the shower we took together to clean up, I was able to focus on her and only her, bringing her to another orgasm with my lips and tongue, washing her without giving in to the temptation to bury myself in her slick, tight flesh.

Though she didn't complain about it this morning, I know she must be sore after yesterday.

And I fucking took her again today.

I drag in a breath and curl my hand into a fist to prevent myself from reaching for her. As much as I want to inspect every inch of her skin to make sure the hickey and the whisker burns are the worst of it, I don't want to wake her. Above all, she needs to rest and heal, to let her body recover from the ordeal it's endured.

She fought a brutal battle with cancer, and she won —and I'll do whatever it takes to ensure she never has to fight another one. I will oversee her diet, hire the best personal trainers and yoga instructors, purge our environment of any and all toxins, and generally go batshit crazy to keep her healthy and well.

And, crucially, not pregnant.

I again didn't wear a condom in the kitchen, so even though the timing is in our favor, I will call her doctors and ask if it's safe for Alina to take a morning-after pill. And going forward, I will stash condoms in every drawer and wall nook, all over the shower and on the fucking ceiling, so I'll hopefully remember to grab one the next time I lose my head around my wife. And if I keep forgetting, I'll get a fucking vasectomy.

In fact, I might as well sign up for one now given how little self-control I have.

I watch her for another moment, drinking in everything about her, and then I go to the bedroom so I can call Alina's doctor about the morning-after pill. Afterward, I'll reach out to my doctor about scheduling a vasectomy. Before I can place the first call, however, my phone screen lights up with an incoming videocall request.

It's Katya, my father's hospice nurse.

My chest ices over.

This is it.

He's dead.

It's over.

Steeling myself, I swipe to accept the call—only to regret it instantly.

As soon as the video fills my screen, Katya's broad mien disappears, replaced by *his* face.

His gaunt, aged-by-three-decades-in-three-months, but unmistakably *alive* face.

I move to disconnect, but my father is already speaking.

"Alexei..." His voice is an agonized rasp. It's shocking he can say anything at all given that the cancer has spread to his vocal cords as well as just about every organ in his body. "Please, son... listen to me. Let me explain."

Despite myself, I hesitate, my finger hovering over the disconnect button. There's nothing he can say, no explanation he can give to heal the Grand Canyon-sized rift that formed between us the moment I read Ksenia's diary and realized my father was even more of a monster to his family than to his enemies. Yet I still fucking hesitate, my stomach roiling as I stare at the screen, struck by what cancer has done to the strong, brutal man who'd loomed so large in my childhood and early adolescent years, by the way it has laid waste to him, diminishing him to this skeletal, dying creature anyone would pity.

Once upon a time, I feared this man.

I respected him.

I even fucking loved him despite the mixture of neglect and iron-fisted discipline that had been his parenting style.

Maybe a part of me is still stuck in that mode because instead of hanging up like I should, I move my finger to the edge of my phone and let him speak.

Chapter 20

Alina

I'm killing the first-level boss for the third time when distant voices enter my consciousness. The boss dissolves in front of me as if I've executed the most advanced maneuver—which I haven't—and I growl in frustration, eyes popping open.

Oh.

I'm on the couch.

That was a dream, not a bug in my code.

The voices that woke me are still there, speaking quietly somewhere nearby. The kitchen, most likely. As I rub the remnants of sleep out of my eyes, I recognize the deep timbre of Alexei but not that of the other man.

We have company.

Crap. Did Alexei have a chance to clean up in the kitchen? It was a mess when we left it, shards of dishes all over the floor and everything. If the guest saw it, he must know what went down… unless he's decided that Alexei and I had a knock-down, drag-out fight.

I'd almost rather he think that.

Face burning, I rise from the couch, only to wince again at the pulling soreness inside. It's worse than this morning, which makes sense given that we had sex again. On the kitchen table.

After I admitted that I want to stay.

I swallow and glance down at myself, not ready to deal with the implications of that. Instead, I focus on my clothes—which are not the least bit company appropriate.

I'm dressed in a pair of fuzzy gray sweatpants and a matching sweatshirt that I found among the new clothes Alexei got for me. I chose them both because my skin felt dry after my second shower of the day, and because I associate video games with comfort. As a young teen, I practically lived in sweats, much to my mom's consternation.

But that was back then. Now I'm a grown woman and Alexei's wife, and I should look presentable at all times.

I creep toward the bedroom as quietly as I can, but they must hear me anyway. The voices fall silent. A second later, footsteps sound in the hallway, and Alexei enters the living room, followed by a tall, steely-eyed man I recognize as his head of security—Chekhov, I believe.

Oops. Too late.

Sheepishly, I meet Alexei's gaze—and forget all about my appearance.

I've never seen his face so dark, his eyes so... hellishly bleak.

My stomach plummets.

Did something happen? Did someone die?

Instinct propels me across the room, toward Alexei, but before I can ask him anything, he turns to Chekhov and says curtly, "You know what to do for now. We'll figure out the rest tonight."

The man nods and disappears down the hallway. A moment later, I hear the elevator doors slide shut.

He's gone. We're alone.

"How are you feeling?" Alexei asks before I can question him. His voice softens, his gaze losing some of the bleakness as it travels over me. "Did you get some rest?"

I wave that away with an impatient hand. "Are *you* okay? Did something happen?"

He stills, an expressionless mask falling over his features. "Such as?" His tone is exaggeratedly bland.

I narrow my eyes. "You tell me." A thought occurs to me, and I gasp out loud. "Is it my brothers? Did they do something?"

He sighs, his expression softening again. "No, Alinyonok. It's nothing like that. It's... family stuff."

His family, he means. Which I'm apparently not considered a part of.

The hurt that spears me is as sharp as it is illogical. It shouldn't matter if he doesn't trust me enough to confide in me about Leonov family matters. We've only just moved past being enemies to... whatever we are now. Until today, I couldn't even admit that I want to be with him, so why should I be surprised that he's not ready to tell me every deep, dark secret?

Then again, maybe he'll never tell me. Maybe that's not the kind of relationship he's envisioning for us. As he's demonstrated over the past few weeks, he definitely wants me and cares about me, but he might see me more as a pretty pet to cuddle than a life partner to share problems with.

I swallow the bitterness coating my tongue at the thought. "Okay. I understand."

I'm about to turn away when he speaks. "You don't. And I don't want you to." His voice is hard.

I nod, trying to ignore the irrational pang of hurt. "Because you don't know me that well yet. Or trust me. I get it."

"Because you don't need even more reasons to hate me or my family," he says harshly, and before I can react to that bombshell, he leans down and places a tender kiss on my forehead, then steps back. "I'm going to take a walk to clear my head, okay? I'll see you in a—"

"Wait!" I grab his arm. "Take me with you."

He frowns. "Alinynok, you're not—"

"I'm well enough, I promise. And I've been so, so cooped up." It's not a lie. After the nap, I feel sufficiently energetic, and I have been stuck indoors since... well, since I met Birgit and she took me in. "Please, Alexei, I'd *kill* for a walk."

Alexei's eyebrows rise, and I pull my hand back, my stomach twisting as I realize what I've said. Between being rushed into surgery and the grueling treatment protocol that followed, I've managed not to think too much about the man whose throat I slit, but I haven't forgotten him.

He has featured prominently in more than one of my nightmares over the past few weeks.

My face must reflect what I'm thinking because Alexei clasps my shoulders in a firm grip and says, "Do not go there. It was self-defense at its most basic. He attacked *you*, remember?"

I take a deep breath and nod. I've been telling myself that as well, and it helps, but not entirely. I still took a life. That man, potential rapist or not, had been someone's son, brother, friend. Even now, there must be people mourning him.

Alexei's eyes narrow on my face. "You're still thinking about that piece of shit, aren't you?" Before I can reply, he sighs and says, "Listen, your brothers and I didn't tell you this because we didn't want to stir up any bad memories in case you'd moved on, but you did the world a favor by getting rid of him. That night, you wouldn't have been that fucker's first victim. He was accused of rape twice in the past five years."

"What?" That goes so far beyond the "pervy idiot" description Birgit gave me. "Why wasn't he in jail then?"

"Because his father has some connections in the local law enforcement, and they were able to spin it as the girl being too drunk or high to be reliable. Each time, the charges were dropped."

I drag in a breath, my head spinning from the new information when Alexei says, "You know what? Let's go for that walk—we could both use a change of scenery. But we turn back the second you get the least bit tired."

And just like that, I get another taste of freedom.

CHAPTER 21

ALEXEI

Alina insists on changing before leaving the house, and I don't object. I love the way she looks in her lounge clothes, all cozy and comfortable, with her beautiful face completely bare, but I know she likes to dress up. Besides, it's getting cold out, so she needs to wear something warm.

So I wait while pacing around the living room, doing my best to think about all the ways I'll fuck her tonight instead of dwelling on the soul-crushing call with my father and his agonized plea at the end. Normally, this strategy would work only too well, but I'm too wound up right now, too much on edge to concentrate on anything but the poisonous cocktail of fury and guilt swirling inside me.

I lied to Alina. It isn't a walk I need but a hard, bloody fight. And not with my guards—I need them all intact for what I'm sure the Molotovs are planning. An underground MMA gym was going to be my destination but no longer. Since Alina is coming with me, it has to be an actual walk. A leisurely lakefront stroll instead of the no-holds-barred, grueling battle that would've let me work off some of the toxic rage burning me up inside.

Finding my hands clenched, I take a breath and slowly let it out as I consciously uncurl my fingers.

I'm not the only one who needs to get out of my head, and if a walk helps Alina take her mind off what happened in that piece-of-shit hostel, it's the least I can do.

It's my fault this happened to her. I should've been there to protect her, to keep her safe.

Just like I should've kept my sister safe all those years ago.

Fuck.

I slam the door on that thought before it can cause the rage to boil over.

Now is not the time to think about Ksenia and my father. Not when I have no outlet for the violence bubbling inside me. I would never in a million years hurt Alina, but the strangers we meet today might not be so lucky if I don't get a hold of myself.

Finally, she emerges from the bedroom—and I forget about everything but her.

She's wearing a cream-colored sweater-dress that falls to the middle of her calves and hugs her slim curves in a way that sends all my blood rushing down south. She's topped it with a beige leather jacket lined with shearling, and on her feet is a pair of brown riding boots. But it's her face that steals my breath: her plush, soft lips are once again painted red, her jade eyes are smoky and mysterious, and her porcelain skin shimmers with a subtle peach tint on the apples of her cheeks.

She's so fucking gorgeous it's unreal.

Finally finding my tongue, I tell her so, and a pretty flush adds more color to her face as she rubs her hand over her short hair.

"Even with this?" she asks with a wry smile.

"Especially with that."

As beautiful as her long hair was, it stole some focus from the striking perfection of her features. Now there's nothing to distract the eye from the stunning symmetry of her bone structure and the sensual lushness of her lips. Not that I'd object if she grew out her hair again—she can do whatever she wants with her appearance.

No makeup, clothing, or hairstyle can change how utterly addicted I am to my wife.

Who, it seems, is finally warming up to me.

That thought is like a soothing balm over the raw anger inside me, and I calm further when Alina casually rests her hand on the crook of my elbow as we exit the building and head down the street. My guards follow, some discreetly, others less so. More of them are stationed throughout the neighborhood, snipers strategically positioned at windows and on roofs, ready for anything—such as an assault by Alina's brothers, whom I don't trust one bit. I'm armed to the teeth as well, just in case.

As we walk through the tourist-packed streets toward the waterfront, I ask Alina if there are any places she particularly likes in the city, given that she's been here before. She tells me about a coffee shop she enjoys, and we stop by there to get a pastry and a cup of matcha latte—the latter with oat milk, as per her new diet plan. The pastry is not on the approved foods list, but the dietician said that occasional treats are okay, and I figure this falls into that category. I get one for myself as well, along with a black coffee, and we consume it all while strolling along Promenade du Lac and debating the merits of the Alps in the summer versus the winter.

It's the closest thing to a date I've had with my wife, and I'm not surprised to find myself enjoying the fuck out of it. This is what our courtship should've been like, what I'd envisioned when I arranged our betrothal. I figured as our official engagement announcement approached, we'd get to know each other by going out to dinner and the movies, hitting up museums and art galleries, all the normal things. But Alina's attitude toward me and our union, combined with her brothers' hatred of my family, made it impos-sible, as did the awful tragedy of her parents' deaths when she was nineteen. From that point on, all I could do was hope that once I made her my wife, she'd come around. And now that it's looking like she has, I'm over the fucking moon—or I would be, if not for the lingering discordant echo in my mind after the conversation with my father.

I do my best to forget it as we continue on, discussing everything from the latest happenings in Moscow to the progress Slava has made with his English. Hearing about the latter is bittersweet for me. I miss my nephew. I wish I could see him grow up instead of hearing about it secondhand. Maybe one day, Nikolai will bring him to Moscow for a visit, and I'll see him in person again. The odds of them inviting me to Nikolai's compound in Idaho after my forcible retrieval of Alina are somewhere between zero and negative ten.

We've just stopped by a monument to watch a yacht pass by when an unfamiliar female voice calls out, "Alina?"

I whip my head around to see a tall, lanky blonde with facial piercings staring at us with wide blue eyes from some dozen meters away.

"Alina?" she repeats, coming toward us, and I realize who she is. I saw her in the footage my security team pulled up after the incident in the hostel.

It's the young woman Alina stayed with when she ran away, the one she told me was *not* a witness to Alina's self-defense efforts—a fact the cameras confirmed by showing her leaving the hostel an hour prior.

"Birgit?" Alina exclaims, extricating her hand from my elbow and switching to English. "I had no idea you were still in town!"

"And I had no idea you were here either. You just up and disappeared on me!" She sounds way more accusing than the length of their acquaintance warrants, and I narrow my eyes as I observe their interaction.

While Alina was recovering after the surgery, I had my security team look into this woman, and off-hand, I don't recall anything too concerning in her file—though there was a mention of a brief relationship with a girl in college.

Could that be it?

Did she view my wife as more than a potential friend?

Motherfucker. Did something *happen* between them in that dingy hotel room?

"Oh, fuck. Your hair..." Birgit sounds shocked as she stops in front of us—close enough for me to slice open her carotid artery with the blade in my pocket. Her gaze jumps to my face for the first time, and she blanches at whatever she sees there, smartly backing up a couple of steps. But she regroups quickly, refocusing on Alina. "That diagnosis you mentioned..." Her gaze drops to Alina's stomach. "Are you—"

"Not anymore." Alina's voice thickens, and the jealous fury flaring within me sputters and dies, smothered by a hollow ache.

This stranger knows about it all. The cancer and the

pregnancy that never was. The baby that was never meant to be, the one Alina had been so convinced was a girl.

I've done my best to move past it, but the images still come to me at night, pulling me out of what little sleep I manage—the tears on Alina's face when she told me she was bleeding, the deathly pallor of her skin when the doctors informed us that the embryo had never truly existed. Worst of all is the knowledge that it's all my fault. That it all happened because I wanted to tie her to me once and for all, to bind us together as irrevocably as two people can be bound.

Some primitive, irrational part of me still wants it, a child that would be hers and mine—even as fear of what a pregnancy could do to her is front and center in my mind.

"I'm sorry," Birgit says softly, and I force myself to focus on her and the potential danger she represents instead of the sucking emptiness in my chest.

Even if her relationship with my wife was exactly as Alina presented it—just a kind stranger helping out— the body Valery's forensic team disposed of makes me wish she'd disappeared from Alina's life for good. Here in Western Europe, the Molotovs and the Leonovs don't have the same pull as we do in Russia, so it's not entirely impossible that Alina would be questioned if some overzealous, too-righteous-for-bribes detective figured out that she was one of the last people to have seen the missing man alive.

Because he *is* missing, as far as the police are

concerned. The Molotovs made sure his body would never be found. They also wiped any and all security footage that placed Alina anywhere near that hostel. The only thing linking her to the dead man is the woman standing in front of me.

Who now knows that Alina is still here in Geneva.

Alina chooses that very moment to look up at me, and the way she pales tells me that I'm not hiding my thoughts well.

"Don't you dare," she whisper-hisses at me in Russian before pasting on a big smile and turning to Birgit while demonstratively grabbing my arm in a possessive, wifely hold. "Sorry, I'm being so rude," she exclaims in a practiced, social-butterfly tone. "Birgit, this is my husband, Alexei Leonov. Alexei, this is my friend, Birgit. She was very kind to me in those terrible days right after my diagnosis."

The smile that stretches my lips holds zero warmth. "A pleasure."

I don't know what the fuck my wife is playing at, but now this woman knows my full name—and by default, Alina's.

Birgit gives me a wary nod. "Likewise." Her eyes flit back to Alina's head and the scars decorating it before she bites her lip and asks tentatively, "How are you… you know?"

"All good," Alina says, a shade too brightly. "Had surgery to remove the tumor, followed by some radiation and immunotherapy, and just got an all-clear. Didn't even need to do a full shave, as it turns out, but I kind of like it." She rubs her head with a self-deprecating smile.

I'm considering what kind of accident could take Birgit out in the near future without Alina finding out and getting upset when Birgit says, "Yeah, looks great on you." Her gaze flicks to me again. "Though I'm sure your husband misses your long hair."

My jaw tightens. "And why's that?"

She shrugs with a cynical half-smile. "All men seem obsessed with that shit." She touches her own short blond locks.

Alina speaks up before I can eviscerate her friend—verbally for now, given that we're in public. "Not this one," she says, squeezing my arm, and when I glance at her, she's gazing up at me with a smile. An *adoring* smile.

It's the first time I've seen such an expression on her face, and it sucks all the breath out of my lungs.

I forget all about Birgit and the herds of tourists milling around us, my heart thudding violently against my ribs as I soak in that gorgeous, radiant smile. It's like tasting sunlight. Like stepping into a warm bath after a Siberian winter night.

I'm fucking destroyed, utterly *dazzled*, and it's only when my wife turns her face away from me and says in a too-sweet, utterly un-Alina-like voice, "You have no idea how amazing Alexei has been to me," that it dawns on me that it's an act.

The same act she puts on around her family to

convince them she doesn't need rescuing—or, more likely, to make me think she's convincing them.

The realization is like downing a shot of acid.

I don't know why Alina cares what this woman thinks of me and our relationship, but she's putting on that act for her as well, only dialed up tenfold… to a level that no one who truly knows her and our history would believe. But presumably, Birgit doesn't know the latter, and thus Alina is trying to convince her that we're something other than what we are.

That we're what I've always wanted us to be.

Suddenly, I see the day through an entirely new lens. Is Alina putting on an act with *me*? Like she did the day she slipped out of that bathroom window after willingly embracing me? Motherfucker… The progress I've been making with her, our newfound comradery— is it all in my head? Her reluctant admission that she wants to stay—was that real or an attempt to manipulate me, to get me to lower my guard so she can… what? Run away again when I'm not looking?

She has to know I won't be that careless again.

No. The more likely possibility is that her brothers are getting ready to do something, and she knows it. Despite my careful monitoring of all her communications, they've somehow managed to convey their plan to her, and she's doing her best to facilitate it… say, by getting us outside into crowded tourist areas, where we're less protected than at my heavily guarded penthouse.

Fuck.

Blocking out Birgit's response to Alina's gushing praise of me, I sweep my gaze over our surroundings. Nothing out of the ordinary. Only my men, holding their positions at strategic distances from us. They appear alert, undistracted—exactly as they should be. Back at the penthouse, the rest of the security team is watching us via street cameras and satellites. No one should be able to get a jump on us, no matter how well-trained and well-armed they are... as the Molotovs' strike team would be.

Still, even once I turn my attention back to the conversation between the two women, the paranoia gnaws hard at me. Because if the Molotovs were going to attempt something, it would be here and now, after Alina got the all-clear but before we went back to Moscow, where my security measures are even stronger.

"—leaving for Thailand soon," Birgit is saying when I tune back in. "A friend of mine moved to Chiang Mai last year, and she loves the climate, the people, everything. You guys should come visit once I settle in. Lots of Russians there, I hear."

"Oh, yes, I've been several times," Alina says animatedly. "I love Chiang Mai, and Krabi is straight-up paradise." She looks up at me. "Alexei, you've been there too, right?"

"Yes." I don't elaborate. The spot between my shoulder blades is itching as if a sniper's laser is dancing over it, and I'm not about to ignore the sensation that's saved my life more than once. I force a reasonably polite smile in Birgit's direction and loop my arm around Alina's back. "Nice meeting you, Birgit. We should get going now."

Before my wife can protest, I guide her away from the crowds.

Paranoia or not, we're going back to the penthouse, where I can keep her safe.

CHAPTER 22

____

ALINA

I'm still fuming at Alexei when we enter the penthouse. We were having _such_ a nice outing, and I was just about to get Birgit's number so we could stay in touch when Alexei abruptly went all cold and dragged me away, not even letting me say goodbye. The only reason I didn't put up a fight was because I didn't want Birgit to think that Alexei was abusive to me or whatever it was she initially suspected at the hostel.

In general, she seems to have a low opinion of men, and I don't want to feed into it. Once things settle down further, I'm hoping to invite her to Moscow for a visit, or to go see her in Thailand, if that's where she ends up.

For now, though, I need to figure out what happened to have Alexei acting so rudely and—

"Hey." Ruslan materializes out of the kitchen,

causing my pulse to jump. Before I can fully register his grim expression, he says, "It's over. He's dead."

My stomach drops. At my side, Alexei freezes. When he speaks a beat later, his voice is hoarse. "But I spoke to him today. Just hours ago."

Ruslan nods, his jaw tight. "So did I. He called me from Katya's phone. I thought she was calling to… you know."

Alexei stabs his fingers through his hair. "Same."

I suck in a breath. Their father. They're talking about Boris Leonov.

He's dead.

My anger deflates, my grievances suddenly petty in light of Alexei and Ruslan's loss. And it *is* a loss, however tense their relationship with their father seemed to be. I can see it on their faces—Alexei's, especially. The tight set of his shoulders and the emptiness in his gaze speaks volumes to me. Without thinking, I reach over and clasp his hand in both of mine, seeking to alleviate his hurt in any way I can.

His gaze swings to me, but there's no warmth in it. His hand is stiff in mine, his fingers cold. I squeeze his palm anyway. I know how pain can be so vast it makes you numb, how grief can smother everything, stamping out every emotion until you feel like you are dead yourself. Like you don't exist.

Like you don't *deserve* to exist.

"The funeral is set for tomorrow evening," Ruslan says. "I'm making the arrangements. You'll be there, right?"

Alexei's hand is still cold in mine, his fingers unbending in my grip. "We're flying back first thing tomorrow, so yes."

"Chekhov filled me in," Ruslan says. "I'm going to fly separately tonight. Just in case."

I blink. In case of what? But Alexei seems to understand because he nods and says, "See you at the funeral."

Without another word, Ruslan heads for the elevator. As he walks past us, I touch his arm and murmur, "I'm sorry."

He flashes me an indecipherable look. "Thanks." He steps into the elevator, and the doors slide shut behind him, leaving us alone.

I turn my full attention to Alexei, who's stepped away to remove his jacket and boots. I remove mine as well. My chest aches for him and Ruslan, for the ordeal that's still ahead of them. Because the death of a loved one is just the beginning. What awaits them is the funeral, the sorting of the belongings, and all the other painful things that go along with the end of a life. I was in no shape to handle that after my parents' traumatic passing, so my brothers took on that burden. I heard them talking about it quietly, when they thought I was asleep or drugged. I heard the strain in their voices, the stress that no amount of wealth or power can shield you from.

My brothers stepped in for me, but there's no one who can step in for Alexei and Ruslan. Their sister is gone as well—another loss they've recently endured.

I wasn't there to help him with his grief then—we were still enemies at that point—but I can be now. The way he was there for me during my battle with cancer.

The way he would've been there for me after my parents' deaths... if I'd let him.

The thought ambushes me, cutting into me like a butcher's knife. And for the first time, I let myself wonder about the "what ifs." What if I hadn't sent Alexei away when he brought me home after my one-and-only shrink visit? What if I'd leaned on him in my trauma and grief instead of pushing him away and relying on the pills?

What if I'd gone with him that awful winter evening instead of returning home to find my parents in the middle of their last, deadly fight? Would the outcome of that fight have been different if I hadn't been there? Would my mother have ended up with bruises and maybe a broken jaw instead of getting slashed beyond recognition by the blade that *I* used to attack my father in order to help her?

Bile fills my throat, and it takes everything I have to swallow it down and force back the tears stinging my eyes. I can't think about all of that now, or I'll unravel. This isn't about me—it's about Alexei and *his* pain, *his* loss and grief.

Drawing in a steadying breath, I cross the room and do what I wanted to do when I heard about his sister's accident.

I wrap my arms around his waist and hold him tight.

His powerful body goes stiff. For several long moments, his arms remain at his sides, unmoving. But then he wraps them around me, hugging me so tightly air vacates my lungs. Bending his head, he presses his face against my hair, and a shudder ripples through him, his own breath exiting in an audible exhale. His familiar pine-and-leather scent surrounds me, and the rough stubble on his jaw scrapes against my temple, a grounding, masculine abrasion in the midst of the silent storm of his grief.

We stand like that, holding each other, for a minute or two. Maybe ten. Time melts away, like ice dissolving on windows in the spring. There are no words I can say to lessen his pain, but I can do this—I can lend him the physical warmth of my body, the animal comfort of my embrace. I can give him at least a fraction of the support he's given me in recent weeks.

The support he would've always given me if I'd accepted it, I now realize.

When he finally pulls away, everything feels different. Not resolved, not fixed—nothing that simple. We're just more... attuned to each other in some subtle way.

Silently, we walk together to the bedroom. I hold his gaze as I undress, and I see the bleakness in his eyes transform into dark, volcanic heat. Once, I would've been frightened by it—and by my body's irrepressible response to it—but no longer. He's taught me to crave it. To crave *him*. Or maybe that craving has always been there, so potent and uncontrollable that the only way to fight the violent pull of it was to reject it altogether, to run as far away from it—and thus from him—as I could.

Maybe the reason he always scared me was not his family's reputation or the darkness I could sense in him, but the way everything about him drew me in from the moment we met, back when I was just barely fourteen… too young to handle that overwhelming pull without losing myself to it.

Maybe I won't be able to handle it even now, but I'm willing to try.

When I'm naked, I reach for his clothes. He lets me push up his T-shirt, exposing his flat, ridged stomach, but he has to be the one to pull the shirt off over his head since I can't reach that high. What I can do is lean in and tongue his small, masculine nipple as soon as his hard-muscled, tattooed chest is bared. Simultaneously, I work on his belt buckle, purposefully rubbing my hand over the hard, massive bulge in his jeans in the process.

At the first touch of my tongue, his breath catches, a low groan rumbling in his throat as he grips my head to keep my mouth pressed against his chest. Encouraged, I graze his nipple with my teeth and then suck on it, and he shudders all over, his hips jerking violently to push his jean-clad erection harder against my hand as he swears explosively, uttering Russian curses so filthy that my face burns and liquid heat streaks down my body.

Seeking more of that response, I switch my attention to his other nipple, but he's not having it. Instead, he guides my head lower, to where I've just managed to unzip him.

"Suck it," he orders in a raspy voice, pulling out his cock with one hand while holding my head with the other, and I gladly fall to my knees, wrapping my lips around the thick, smooth column.

Unlike the time he fucked my mouth back on the yacht, he's gentle. Careful. Even as the vibrating tension of his muscles betrays his raw desperation, he makes sure not to press on the still-healing scars on my head or to otherwise cause me any discomfort. He lets me set the pace, to lick and stroke and suck him as I wish, and I revel in the freedom of it, in my ability to please him, to drive him as mad as he drives me. Every groan I elicit, every involuntary thrust of his hips, is a small victory, though I no longer know in which war.

All I know is that he's magnificent like this, a stunning male animal lost in lust, his powerful muscles bunching and quivering from the effort of restraining himself, his throat corded as he throws his head back with a stifled groan and pours his cum down my throat.

I swallow it all and lick him clean, a part of me disappointed it's over so quickly. Except it's not. Even after his orgasm, he's barely softened, and by the time I'm done cleaning him off, his cock is fully rigid again, thick and massive, ready for more.

Ready for me.

Always ready for me.

"Come here," he says hoarsely, pulling me to my feet, and what follows is the closest we've ever gotten to making love. He explores and worships every part of my body, finding erogenous areas I didn't even know I possessed—like the backs of my knees and the undersides of my breasts. I come twice before he enters me, and when he does, he fucks me so tenderly it makes me want to weep. And I come again. And again. Until I'm utterly wrung out yet unwilling to close my eyes for fear that this is just a dream, that if I fall asleep and wake up, we'll be back to what we were instead of... what we are becoming.

So I stay awake even as the light fades outside, day transitioning smoothly into night. Lying on my side, I trace circles on his chest, studying his intricate dragon tattoos in the dim light of the bedside lamp he's flipped on, and we still don't speak. Not really. Nothing beyond a few sex words and my reassurances that I'm okay, that I'm still not too tired... though I definitely am.

Finally, I break the silence. "So why the dragons?"

I asked him this on the yacht, and he brushed me off with some bullshit answer. I wait to see if he'll do that again, but he sighs and says, "It's stupid. Just a children's fairy tale I used to like."

I lift my head off the pillow to look at him. "What kind of fairy tale?"

He's staring at the ceiling, not meeting my gaze. "A

generic one. Nothing special, really. My mother used to read it to me when I was little, and after she was gone, I... read it to myself for a bit."

His mother. My chest squeezes. "What was it about?"

He lets out a huff of air. "Dragons, what else? And a prince and a princess. Like I said, generic and unimaginative. I don't even remember the title of that story."

He's lying again. The story was special to him. Special enough that he's subjected himself to hours upon hours of needle torture to carry it on his skin.

"What did the dragons do?" I ask softly. "Were they heroes or villains in the story?"

"Villains, of course." His dark eyes glint as he turns his head to look at me. "Aren't they always? Their job was to die. The prince needed to slay them in order to win the princess's hand in marriage and her heart."

"Ah. And were they hard to slay?"

"Very." His mouth twists. "It took him many years, but he finally succeeded."

I sit up, holding a corner of the blanket against my chest to keep myself warm. "Did he?"

The glint in his eyes intensifies. "You tell me."

We're not talking about a fairy tale anymore. Maybe we never were.

My first instinct is to avert my gaze, to pretend I don't understand the question. And before today, that's what I might've done. But things are different now. I can no longer see him as the demon who's haunted my life for so long.

He's all too human, his pain and grief all too real. All too familiar to me.

Despite what I've told myself over the years, Alexei Leonov is not a cruel monster. Or at least that's not all he is.

"I…" I inhale deeply, holding his gaze. "Yes. I think he did."

Something moves in his eyes, a peculiar tension tightening his jaw. "Is that right?"

I nod, fighting the urge to look away, to deny the truth. That's what I've done for years. Maybe even for the full decade-plus that we've known each other. I've told myself he's too much like my father, too much like *his* father. Over and over, I've reminded myself that he's ruthless and dangerous, manipulative and obsessive, a lethally possessive killer with no conscience—and he is all of those things. But he's also loyal, and caring, and… *mine*.

The word comes out of nowhere, but as it settles into my mind, I feel the truth of it, the sheer inevitability.

He's *mine*.

My monster.

My demon.

My ruthless stalker.

When I thought he no longer wanted me, it was like being diagnosed with cancer all over again.

So instead of hiding from it, I take a deep breath and say what I haven't dared to admit even to myself.

"I love you, Alexei. I think a part of me has always loved you… even when I thought I hated you. It just took me time to realize it."

And tightening my grip on the blanket, I wait for his response.

CHAPTER 23

ALEXEI

I sit up, my heart slamming painfully against my ribs as I stare at my wife.

Did I just hear that right?

"You love me." My voice comes out flat. Emotionless. As though there isn't a volcanic storm raging inside me, battering my chest with all kinds of contradictory feelings… like violent joy and bitter disbelief.

If she'd told me this yesterday or any other day, I would've been over the fucking moon. This is what I've always wanted, what I've been convinced would eventually happen. But a kernel of doubt was planted on our walk, and even though no attack took place as we hurried home, I still can't help but wonder if everything that's occurred between us since we came back to the penthouse has been part of her plan to get me to lower my guard… including this confession.

Her throat ripples as her fingers tighten on the blanket she's holding up. "Yes. I do."

Fuck. This is tearing me apart. All I want is to embrace her and tell her how much I love her, how I absolutely *adore* her and always fucking have, but the suspicion that she's playing me is like a poisonous seed stuck in my throat. I've already shared too much in the warm afterglow of sex, and what comes to my mind now is how she'd willingly embraced me at the clinic before her treatment, only to slip away right after we'd had sex. How she sought me out at her friend's fundraiser a few weeks after Ksenia's death, allegedly to offer me her sympathy... only to run and hide in Nikolai's Idaho compound immediately afterward.

Is that what's happening here?

Is she giving me something she knows I badly want in order to up her chances of a successful escape?

Did her fucking *brothers* put her up to this?

No. I refuse to believe it. I've always been able to read her; unlike Valery, deception isn't her strong suit. And yet... I can't bring myself to speak, to return the words I know she's waiting to hear.

Instead, I do the only thing I can.

I reach for the blanket she's holding and pull it away, baring her exquisite breasts. Then I give in to the ever-present hunger raging inside me, the desperate need no amount of sex will ever sate.

I show her with my body what I can't tell her with my words, make her come over and over again, and when she's finally worn out and asleep, I hold her tightly as I lie wide awake, my mind cycling through all the possible weak spots in my security arrangements, all the ways she could be taken from me… all the ways I could still lose her.

Like I lost Ksenia.

And my mother.

And now my father.

I shouldn't care about the latter. Even before I learned about Ksenia's terrible secret, we weren't close. So it shouldn't matter, shouldn't hurt, but it does, and I don't fucking know why.

The funeral is tomorrow afternoon. We'll fly out early in the morning, and then we'll be home, the difficult days of Alina's treatment behind us as we start our new life together as a married couple.

It's everything I've always wanted, so why can't I close my eyes and just fucking *sleep*?

———

MY HEAD IS POUNDING AS OUR JET TOUCHES DOWN ON our private airstrip in Moscow. I'd just finally closed my eyes when my alarm went off. The morning flew by in a blur of preparations and coordination with my security team, and then we were off. I was hoping to sleep on the plane, like Alina did, but I was too wound up.

The good news is we've made it to Moscow in one piece. Nobody attacked us on the way to the airport or while we were in the air—not that I was really expecting the latter. The Molotovs wouldn't do anything to endanger their sister, I'm reasonably sure of that. Now we just need to get through the funeral, and I'll finally be able to relax in my own bed.

With Alina.

My wife, who says she loves me.

Fuck. If I could just fully trust her, I—

"Are you okay?" Alina's voice is soft, her eyes filled with sympathy when I meet her gaze.

Since we're heading straight to the funeral, she's already wearing a long-sleeved black dress, her slender, shapely legs clad in opaque black tights that disappear into high-heeled black ankle boots. It's a simple, monochromatic outfit, but my Alinyonok looks amazing in it, as always. Her full lips are once again painted red, her green eyes are lined with the black stuff that makes them especially cat-like, and the paleness of her porcelain skin forms a dramatic contrast with her dark outfit.

"I'm okay," I tell her, reaching over to clasp her slender hand. For now, I choose to believe that this is for real, and if it's not, I'll deal with it like I've dealt with every other obstacle my stubborn wife has thrown in our path.

She puts on a black wool coat, and then we exit the plane and go straight into an armored SUV. From there, it's an hour's drive to the scenic rural area my father chose as his burial site. It's not a cemetery, just a piece of land we own. My mother is buried there too; my father didn't want her to be among random corpses, he told me once.

The same reasoning must apply to himself.

Ruslan is already there when we arrive, having flown in separately from us in case of a Molotov attack. Other attendees include high-ranking officials and politicians, business acquaintances, and various relatives. To my surprise, the latter includes Aunt Sonia, our mother's sister, who must've flown in all the way from Krasnodar. At a glance, I count at least two hundred people, but it could easily be closer to three hundred.

The priest is still getting ready, so I walk around and introduce Alina to key people. I don't know what I expected, but my wife is pleasant and courteous, polite to everyone. There isn't even a hint of the enmity that's existed between our families for so long, nor any sense that she's reluctant to be here, with me.

Real or an act?

Fuck. I can't stop wondering.

Aunt Sonia approaches just as Vitaly Petrov, Moscow's new mayor, is expressing his condolences. I excuse us and go give her a hug. Though she's never been a fan of my father, she's stayed in our lives since my mother's passing, and I'll always be grateful for that.

In some ways, she's been like a second mother to me and Ruslan, and even more so to Ksenia, who spent most of her summers with her in Krasnodar.

Once she releases me from the hug, I introduce her to Alina, who seems slightly taken aback when Aunt Sonia pulls her into a hug as well. But she recovers quickly, and I'm glad to see her smiling warmly at my aunt—who's admittedly a bit much at times.

"Oh, just look at you," Aunt Sonia gushes, clasping Alina's face between her palms as if my wife were a cute toddler. "You're just as beautiful as Alexei has always told me—that short hair is the bomb on you. I'm so glad you're feeling better too! Though you must be so tired after your long flight. You are, aren't you?" She grabs both of Alina's hands in hers. "You poor thing, you haven't even had a chance to rest and change before needing to come here. Are you hungry?" She shifts her grip to Alina's elbow. "Come, there's a nice spread over there—"

"Aunt Sonia." I gently extract my wife from her hold. "Thank you, but we ate on the plane before landing." I glance at Alina. "Unless you'd like something?"

Alina's lips are twitching, as if she's trying to hold back laughter. "I'm okay, thanks."

Aunt Sonia is undeterred. "Well, let's get you a drink. You look positively parched!"

Before Alina or I can protest, she drags her away. I start after them, but Alina catches my gaze and gives a subtle shake of her head. I guess she's okay with this. I sigh and turn a portion of my attention to yet another politician who's come to pay his respects, no doubt in the hopes of securing a juicy contribution to his reelection campaign.

Most of my focus remains on Alina, though.

It always does.

CHAPTER 24

ALINA

It's official. Alexei's aunt has to be the nicest, most exhausting person I've ever met.

She chatters nonstop as she drags me to the drink station, where she proceeds to ply me with everything from fresh-squeezed orange juice—"for the vitamin C, dear!"—to berry-infused black tea and sparkling mineral water. The latter is supposed to "flush out the toxins with the bubbles."

I politely take a few sips of each drink, grateful that she's at least not pushing alcohol. Champagne and vodka are definitely not on the dietician's approved list of beverages. Then again, Sonia seems to know about my cancer; her comments about me "feeling better" indicate as much. I wonder who told her. Alexei? Ruslan? Judging by the way she enthusiastically waved at Ruslan when he passed by, she's close to them both.

It's interesting to observe my husband in this milieu, where he and his brother reign supreme.

Everyone gravitates toward him, but he's cool and distant with them… completely unlike the way he was with the short, plump woman who's currently talking my ear off about her recent trip to the "healing waters" in the Czech Republic—something she's highly recommending I do.

"I'll definitely talk to Alexei about it," I promise with a smile.

She claps her hands. "Yes! It'll be so good for you. And there's an amazing psychic there too. You two should consult her. She's told me all kinds of things over the years, and they've all come true!"

Okay, now she's lost me. But I keep smiling and listening as she tells me how the psychic predicted the exact date her cat would come into her life, and what kind of curses her parrot would learn.

"I swear, I didn't say those words around him, ever, yet he learned them, just like she said he would," she says with amazement in her voice. "And don't even get me started on what she told me about my dog!"

I'm not about to, but she tells me anyway. And I'm glad she does because the story somehow transitions into one about a teenage Alexei cuddling the same dog as a puppy, and my heart goes haywire at the images that fill my mind.

Alexei with a puppy.

Alexei with a baby.

Our baby.

One we may never have.

I don't realize I'm blinking back tears until Sonia

lays her hand on my arm and says softly, "Oh, honey. You have it just as bad as he does, don't you? My psychic said that would be the case. I guess she was right again."

"Your psychic?" I stare at her, distracted. "She told you about… Alexei and me?"

"Of course. She tells me everything." Sonia's hazel eyes shine in her round face. "When Alexei was eighteen, she told me he'd meet a girl soon, and she'd forever be the one for him. Said their path wouldn't be easy, but if they made the right choices, it would all work out in the end."

That's exactly the sort of thing a "psychic" would say—vague and generic, applicable to pretty much anyone. Yet my spine prickles, as if someone has tickled my neck with a feather, and I find myself weirdly hungry for more.

"What exactly did she say?" I ask, and instantly want to kick myself.

Why am I encouraging this madness? I don't believe in psychics or predictions.

Sonia's voice softens, the shine in her gaze dimming. "She told me that Alexei's fated love would have great trauma in her life… that she'd experience a tragedy that would sink its claws not only into her soul but also her flesh."

Chills run down my back, even as I tell myself that Sonia is just saying this because she knows my story. If Alexei or whoever told her about my cancer, they probably also spoke to her about my parents' deaths…

maybe even gave her the full story. Then Sonia blabbed to this con artist, who promptly repackaged it with a profound bullshit wrapper and sold it to her as a so-called prediction.

It's the only explanation that makes sense.

"She also said that she'd either break or emerge stronger from it," Sonia continues. "And that ultimately, she would have to make a choice. As would Alexei."

More vague bullshit. Could the con be more obvious? And yet… "What kind of choice?" I demand.

Sonia shrugs helplessly. "She didn't say."

Of course she didn't. Because she was talking out of her ass, making up the most plausible-sounding thing that could apply to hundreds of different couples and all sorts of situations. Come to think of it, Sonia didn't even need to tell this con woman about my parents.

For most young people, "trauma" and "tragedy" could mean anything from losing a favorite pet to getting rejected from their first-choice college.

Still, as Sonia starts telling me about all the things the psychic predicted about her hamster, I can't help but think about choices.

I've made mine.

Yesterday, I admitted to myself and to Alexei that I love him.

And he didn't say it back.

I'm trying not to dwell on it, to remind myself that he's going through a traumatic loss of his own, his second one in as many years. I tell myself that he's shown and told me in a dozen different ways how he truly feels. Yet a small, insecure part of me can't help but wonder if the reason he didn't say the words was because he didn't want to lie to me.

If, after everything, he's made his choice as well… and I'm not it.

———

I'M STILL RUMINATING ON THE TOPIC WHEN ALEXEI comes to retrieve me. As the service begins, the priest launches into a monologue about what a great man Boris Leonov was, and I only half-listen, all my attention on Alexei.

His expression is remote. Emotionless. Even as his fingers curl tightly around mine, keeping my hand warm in the frigid wind that smells of approaching snow, he doesn't look at me, doesn't acknowledge that I'm there.

I know he's hurting. I feel his pain and grief as if it were my own. But all I can do is stand by his side and hold his hand instead of embracing him as I would if we were alone. That is, if he'd let me embrace him. There seems to be an invisible wall between us, a barrier that I can't penetrate.

I don't understand why it's there. Is it *because* he's hurting? Some kind of tough-man act where he doesn't want to show weakness? Or is it what I said? Did the admission of my feelings, coming as it did after all these years, seem… anticlimactic to him?

Presumably, this was his goal all along: to make me fall in love with him. Everything he's done, all the manipulations, all the blood spilled, has been in service of that. But maybe that's the thing… Maybe the fun was in the chase, not the getting. He could be realizing that he only wanted me for as long as I didn't want him back—or claimed not to.

That he doesn't actually love me and never will.

"How are you feeling, Alinyonok? Are you tired?" Alexei's low-pitched voice cuts into my gloomy thoughts, and I all but jump.

He's looking at me now, his gaze filled with familiar concern. The priest is still speaking, but Alexei doesn't seem to care, his focus on me once more.

A warm glow kindles in my chest, chasing away the insidious doubts. "I'm okay, thank you."

It's mostly true. Though I slept for several hours on the plane, jet lag is pulling at me hard, much harder than it would've in the past. My head feels heavy, my eyes are gritty, and my stomach is unsettled, possibly from all the healthy drinks Sonia forced on me. But I'm nowhere near as exhausted as I would've been even two weeks ago.

"Okay, let me know if you need us to leave. We'll go right away," Alexei says, squeezing my hand, and turns his attention to the priest, who's finally wrapping up.

It's time for family and friends to say a few words, but neither Ruslan nor Alexei move to do so. After an awkward pause, other relatives step up, followed by business associates and whoever else wants to demonstrate their loyalty to the deceased and, by extension, to the remaining Leonov clan.

After each sycophantic speech, I sneak a glance at my husband, but his closed-off expression gives nothing away. That's another reason I feel insecure, I realize—his refusal to tell me anything about his relationship with his father.

Thanks to his accessing of my therapist's files all those years ago—not to mention, a decade of relentless stalking—he knows my family's deepest, darkest secrets, whereas I know next to nothing about his family and the source of their dysfunction.

Finally, the speeches are over, and the post-service mingling begins. By now, I *am* tired. Barely hanging on, in fact.

I'm about to fess up to Alexei, but he beats me to it.

"It's time for us to go," he says, ignoring the people approaching us. "You've had a long day."

With that, he says goodbye to Sonia and a few others and hustles me to the car, where I drift off as soon as I close my eyes.

CHAPTER 25

ALEXEI

Alina is still asleep, her head resting on my shoulder as we pull up to the suburban mansion I built for us. I gently shake her awake, glad we've made it home without any misadventures.

Since the Molotovs didn't try to take her in Geneva, I was fully expecting them to pull something on the way to or from the funeral. I was ready for anything and everything, and they must've known that.

They're waiting for me to lower my guard, probing for weaknesses.

Well, they won't find any.

Alina is mine for good.

Lifting her head off my shoulder, she blinks open her eyes and yawns delicately, covering her mouth with one hand. "We've arrived?" She sounds deliciously sleepy.

I smile and bring her hand to my lips to place a kiss on the back. "We have."

Now that the funeral is over, some of the bitter rage choking me has subsided, though it's not gone by any means. But *she* makes it better. Having her with me at the funeral, touching her, looking at her—it made those awful hours go by faster. I could focus on the warmth of her hand instead of the bullshit praise the priest was spouting off, could think about the way her lips curved softly as she spoke to Aunt Sonia instead of the hollow agony I felt when I looked at the coffin and pictured Ksenia's body in there instead of my father's.

"Good," Alina says softly. She sits up straighter, looking more awake. "I want to see our new home."

Our new home. My pulse skips a beat. Does she mean it? Is that how she truly sees it, or is she saying that to make me believe she loves me?

Fuck. I need to nip this paranoia in the bud. There's no good reason for me to distrust her. Except... her brothers still haven't tried to rescue her.

Why not?

Could they be waiting for her to execute *her* part of the plan? Which involves convincing me that she wants to be with me?

It would be easier for them to take her if I didn't expect her to escape at the first opportunity... if I gave her the freedom my wife would normally have.

Fucking fuck. I need to stop this and just fucking *enjoy* her not fighting me at every step.

"I'll show you around first thing tomorrow," I say as

I help her out of the car. "Tonight, we should get some sleep."

Fuck knows, I need it.

She nods, her brow furrowing as she studies my face. "You look exhausted. When was the last time you slept?"

Real or not, I can't help smiling at the wifely concern in her tone. "It's been a minute. But don't worry, our bed is waiting."

Whether we're going to sleep right away is a different story.

As tired as I am, what I'm looking forward to most is sinking deep inside her and hearing her tell me again that she loves me.

Even if it's a lie.

CHAPTER 26

ALINA

Our new residence is everything I'd expected and more. A strikingly modern slate-gray mansion surrounded by immaculately land-scaped trees that partially hide the sky-high fences surrounding it, it's equal parts fortress and architectural marvel. Extending some dozen meters above ground—and, I bet, deep underground—it boasts a flat roof with raised edges (presumably for the guards to have cover if they're repelling an attack), a front door made of a solid stone slab located deep within a recessed niche, and zero windows. At least as of this moment.

I'm guessing some of the thick walls slide apart to reveal floor-to-ceiling windows when it's deemed safe. Which is apparently not this evening.

As we approach, the stone-slab door retracts side-ways into the wall with a barely audible pneumatic hiss, revealing a foyer that manages to be both imposing and welcoming. The floor is a warm-toned travertine, contrasting with walls paneled in dark, vertically grained wood. Subtle warm light washes down from recessed fixtures, catching the metallic sheen of abstract sculptures placed in rectangular niches. It smells faintly of winter pine and expensive leather, a scent that reminds me of Alexei himself.

A wide archway leads into the main living area. Cathedral-height ceilings arc high above polished concrete floors that are warmed by vast deep-pile rugs in charcoal gray. While one wall is indeed a massive, unbroken surface that likely hides the windows, the others feature integrated shelving units displaying curated objects d'art and strategically placed panels that probably conceal screens or weapon safes.

As Alexei shepherds me through the space toward a glass-and-chrome staircase in the left corner, I notice that the furniture is modern with a cozy vibe—deep sofas upholstered in rich velvet paired with sleek armchairs and glass tables. I also spot small, almost invisible sensors integrated into the ceiling corners, their dark lenses blending seamlessly.

I tear my gaze from them, only to find myself captured by the intense look on Alexei's face. He's watching me, assessing my reaction to our surroundings, and the naked hunger in his eyes makes my breath stall in my lungs. All of a sudden, I become aware of the warmth emanating from his strong hand that rests on the small of my back, of the way he's subtly but determinedly forcing me to move faster as we reach the top of the stairs.

My pulse jacks up, a familiar fire rushing over my skin. Invisible wall or not, he wants me. There's no doubt about that. Not with the dark heat in his eyes and the coiled tension in his powerful body.

The moment we're in the bedroom, he's going to pounce.

A pulsing ache starts between my thighs at the thought, and I find my steps speeding up. And then we're there, inside the bedroom, and his hands are on me, tearing at my clothes, at his clothes.

With ruthless efficiency, he strips us both naked, then picks me up and carries me to the massive bed in the center of the room, the heat of his body warming me in the cool air. As he walks, I catch a glimpse of movement and realize the wall to my right is a full-wall mirror.

Startled, I glance around.

The opposite wall is mirrored as well, as is the ceiling.

We're everywhere, our reflections like a live porn stream.

It's disconcerting. And hot.

Alexei is huge compared to me, all hard, flexing muscle and raw male strength. His inked skin is a dark, intricate tapestry against my paleness. In the mirrors, the coiling dragons on his chest and arms seem to multiply, surrounding me, branding me as property of my demonic lover.

I look small, disturbingly fragile in his embrace, yet I don't feel unsafe, not even when my eyes return to his and I see the feral hunger on his face.

Our sex may be rough at times, but he will never truly hurt me… not like my father hurt my mother.

I feel it with bone-deep certainty.

He deposits me onto the bed, and before I can do anything, he spreads my knees apart and buries his head between my legs, ravenously lapping at my folds. I gasp, arching up as the warm, wet strokes of his tongue electrify my nerve endings, skyrocketing the tension building inside me.

Panting, I fist the sheets, my gaze glued to the erotic tableau in the ceiling mirror as the orgasm rushes at me like a high-speed train, the sensations cresting suddenly and violently, making me convulse with pleasure.

"Again," he says hoarsely, not lifting his head, and I feel the thick, prodding pressure of his finger pushing into me. No, two fingers. The stretch is almost too much, but also somehow not enough. I squirm, crying out as an aftershock makes me clench around the invasive digits, and then his tongue returns, wet and soft, dragging over my pulsing clit as his fingers curl inside me, rubbing against my G spot with unerring precision.

I combust again, the second orgasm so sudden and intense it paints my vision white and wrenches another cry from my throat. The sharp throb of pleasure doesn't end; his fingers stay inside me, pressing and rubbing, pushing me toward the edge again, not letting me catch my breath. I squeeze my eyes shut as he pushes in a third finger, and the stretching sensation intensifies, edging into pain. But it feels good too, especially with his hot, wet tongue lapping at my clit, the soft, slick stroking contrasting with the rough invasion of his fingers.

I come again. Maybe. Or maybe it's the never-ending aftershocks that make my toes curl and my breath exit on a gasp.

And then I gasp again, clenching hard against a new sensation.

A finger of his other hand is probing at my back entrance, using the wetness from my orgasms and his saliva to push into my ass, slowly but inexorably, advancing a millimeter at a time.

My heartbeat quadruples, scorching heat rushing over me, making me feel dizzy. The sensation is so strange, so foreign and... and *wrong* that my eyes pop open and I arch off the bed again, gripping his hair instead of the sheets. The dark locks feel thick and silky between my fingers as I tug on them, trying to pull his head away.

"Alexei..." My voice is breathless and a little panicked. "What... are you doing?"

He lifts his head to look at me, but he doesn't remove his fingers—not the three in my pussy and not the one that's slowly penetrating my ass. His lips are wet and shiny, his coal-black eyes gleaming with possessive hunger.

"Don't worry, Alinyonok…" His voice is a low, dark croon. "I'll make it good for you, I promise."

And if I don't want you to?

I'm tempted to ask, but I don't know if I want to know the answer. Would he stop if I told him to? And… would I *want* him to stop if I said so? Because maybe, just maybe, a tiny, deeply unfeminist part of me likes the imbalance in our relationship, the one that gives him all the power, all the agency… all the responsibility.

No, that's crazy. And yet, I don't ask the question. I don't speak at all—partially because I can't. As Alexei lowers his head and resumes licking my folds, I'm overwhelmed by the sensations, bombarded with a mix of intense pleasure and growing discomfort, the burning stretch in that part of me where entry feels so wrong. It's just his finger, but it's still too much, too invasive, a strange, too-full feeling that makes me squirm and gasp, clenching tightly against the steadily advancing pressure.

"Relax," Alexei urges hoarsely. "Push out…" And when I attempt to do so, he breathes, "Yes, just like that… Let me in… Good girl."

His finger is all the way inside my ass now. Combined with the three in my pussy, it feels like I'm stuffed to the brim, so full I'm about to burst from it. It's odd, and uncomfortable, and… a perverse turn-on, especially with the attention he's paying to my oversensitive clit. Panting, I clench again—and then, with a keening cry, I come, fireworks exploding in my core and dancing over my skin, leaving me shaken and breathless, so limp and drained I'm barely conscious.

But Alexei is not done with me yet. Leaving his finger in my ass, he moves up over me and claims my lips with a fierce kiss before entering me with his cock. The usual thick stretch from his shaft is exacerbated by the foreign sensation of that finger, and I shudder, my inner muscles spasming as aftershocks from the orgasm assail me, one after another. The squeezing sensation must feel good to him because he groans low in his chest and pushes all the way into me, lodging himself so deep that I cry out, digging my nails into his shoulders.

He pulls back halfway and lifts his head. Shakily, I open my eyes and meet his gaze. His eyes are midnight dark, burning into me with ferocious intensity.

"Say it," he demands in a low rasp, and somehow, I know what he wants. What he needs from me.

"I love you." The words spill from my lips like water from an overfilled cup. "I love you, Alexei, with everything I am."

His eyes flare with nuclear heat, and I wait for him to say it back, but he doesn't. Instead, he kisses me again—a deep, rough kiss that devours—and then thrusts back in, starting a slow, steady rhythm. And then... oh, fuck. I forget all about the unsaid words as he begins to move the finger in my ass, in and out, matching the thrusting pace of his cock.

The sensations are unreal, so raw and carnal and intense that my eyes roll into the back of my head, my heart racing dangerously fast as violent heat scorches me from within. It's overwhelming, too much and not enough at the same time, and I hear myself begging, pleading for him to stop—no, to keep going. The tension gathering inside me is enormous, unbearable. It fills my core until I'm vibrating like a plucked string, every muscle in my body taut and straining. I'm on the precipice of something huge, something that's going to shatter me. I know it, I feel it. And then… it's there.

A tsunami of pleasure slams into me, ecstasy erupting in every nerve, every cell. A white glow engulfs my vision, and a cry rips from my throat as I convulse, over and over again, my body spasming around him until, with a guttural groan, he comes, his thick shaft jerking inside me for what feels like an hour.

I'm so thoroughly destroyed that I barely register it when he pulls out of me some time later and disposes of a condom. Hazily, I wonder when he had a chance to put it on, but the thought slips away, my eyes closing of their own accord as exhaustion claims me, dragging me into the land of dreams.

Chapter 27

Alina

My first couple of weeks at our new house are a marathon of unpacking and settling in, in between visits from Alexei's family and mine. Alexei's aunt, Sonia, spends several days in Moscow after the funeral, and we see her almost every day, along with Ruslan, who comes over when she does. By the end of her visit, I've almost gotten used to her eccentricity, and I can't deny that it's fun to observe her relationship with my husband and his brother, both of whom she treats with a bossy sort of affection that must be a leftover from when they were kids.

"I told you to let me make my cabbage soup for Alina," she chides Alexei after I make a face at being offered a salad of dandelion greens for lunch. "It's just what she needs, all the good, healthy—"

"Aunt Sonia." Alexei's tone holds more than a hint of amusement. "You know as well as I do that your cabbage soup is mostly lard."

She bristles. "There's less than a quarter kilo lard in there! How else do you get flavor with cabbage soup if not with lard?"

"So, so many ways," Ruslan mutters, not looking up from his plate, and she swats him on the arm.

"Oh, shut it. I swear, you young people don't know what good cooking is. I mean, what *is* this stuff?" She lifts her fork with a piece of dandelion leaf speared on it. "In my days, we called this a weed." She waves her fork in front of Alexei's face. "Tell me the truth... Did you pluck this on the side of the road?"

"It was grown in the purest organic soil in the best greenhouse in Moscow," Alexei informs her. "Harvested this morning and delivered straight here to ensure maximum freshness." He catches my gaze. "Try it, Alinyonok. It may surprise you."

I heave a sigh. "All right." Kale, I can tolerate, but these bitter greens... Still, I shovel in a forkful of salad, if only to show that I'm on Alexei's side in this argument. I do *not* want to have to eat cabbage soup that's mostly lard; I still have awful memories of my late grandmother, my dad's mom, force-feeding me her version of this Russian classic when I was three or four.

The salad is surprisingly good. The miso-based dressing is sweet and savory, masking the bitterness of the greens, and chunks of orange and avocado lend acidity and creaminess to the dish.

It's as flavorful as anything served in a top restaurant, and I tell Alexei as much.

He squeezes my hand where it rests on the table. "I'm glad you like it. I made it myself."

I'm not surprised—Alexei has been cooking all our meals lately, as if reluctant to entrust my nutrition to anyone else—but Ruslan and Sonia express their disbelief.

"What about the rest of the meal?" Ruslan asks, gesturing at the artfully arranged dishes all over the table. "Surely Vika was involved? She's still your chef, right?"

"She's visiting her family in Chukotka right now," Alexei says. "But yes, when she returns, I expect she'll resume cooking for us."

I'm not so sure that's true. I think Alexei may be enjoying doing this on his own. More than one morning, I've caught him looking up new healthy recipes and tinkering with the ones the dietician provided. I suspect this newfound hobby may be his way of dealing with his worry about my health, especially the fear of my cancer returning—a fear I very much share but am handling by beginning a new, doctor-approved exercise routine and working on my video game.

I also started therapy this week.

I've only had one session so far, so I can't say if it's helped one way or another, but I'm willing to give it a shot. The therapist, an older woman with the kindest face imaginable, got my entire life story out of me during our two-hour initial meeting, and then she assigned me homework—breathing exercises and a very specific kind of journal, one in which I'm supposed to write out my worst fears and what would happen if they came true. I think the idea is to make me see that I'm capable of surviving whatever curveball life throws my way.

The thing is, I already believe that I am. The cancer has left me weaker physically—something I'm working on with the new exercise routine—but mentally, I'm in a better place than I was before the diagnosis. A healthier place. I still experience worry and fear, grief and pain, but I no longer let the negative emotions weigh me down to the point that I need to seek escape in pills.

Maybe it's because that which I once feared most—marriage to Alexei—has turned out to be the best thing in my life.

Every morning, I open my eyes to find him watching me. It's both creepy and exhilarating, this unconcealed obsession of his. I no longer have any doubt that he wants me. He's almost always touching me, even if it's just a casual hand on my knee, and we're rarely apart. Even when I'm deeply absorbed in coding, I'm aware of him casually sitting next to me, busy with his own work. And even though I'm feeling infinitely better these days, he insists on taking care of me, doing everything from cooking for me to helping me unpack and organize all the things I've had moved here from my Moscow penthouse.

Our sex life is also off the charts—not that I'm surprised by that. Now that I'm regaining my health, Alexei seems determined to make up for all those years of abstinence on his part. We have sex multiple times a day, to the point that I'm often sore and aching. At times, it's quick and rough; at other times, it's a tender, drawn-out lovemaking where he worships every part of my body and leaves me a boneless lump in the aftermath. Frequently, he pushes me to my limits and beyond, yet I'm always left craving more at the end. More of the extreme sensations and more of *him*.

Alexei is my new drug, and there's no saving me from this addiction.

My brothers seem determined to try, however. They don't believe me when I tell them, over and over, that I want to stay with him. Each time they visit, they try to get me to give them the green light for whatever plan they've hatched for my "rescue"—a green light that I refuse to give, and not just because I'm afraid of the potential bloodshed, as before.

I simply can't bear the thought of being apart from Alexei... even though he still hasn't told me he loves me.

I try not to let it get to me. After all, some men just have trouble with that word, that very concept. And not just men. If it weren't for my illness, it would've taken me much longer to come around, to accept my feelings and the vulnerability that inevitably accompanies them. Staring my own mortality in the face helped me let go of the decade of denial, of the fear of repeating my mother's errors and enduring her fate.

If I hadn't gotten cancer, Alexei and I might still be at odds with each other. At the very least, it would've been much harder for me to see him as anything more than a cruel puppet master—an aspect of his personality that is still very much there but that I no longer view as solely negative.

If anything, I'm grateful for his machinations now.

After all, they brought us together.

———

BY THE END OF THE THIRD WEEK, WE'RE FULLY SETTLED in, and I invite Natasha to our house for lunch. It's just us girls—Alexei left for a business meeting—and I relish the ability to catch up undisturbed with my childhood friend.

"So, you and Alexei Leonov, huh?" she says after we're done squealing over each other's hairstyles—hers a sleek blond bob, mine now something approaching a cute pixie cut. "I knew it!"

I was leading her to the kitchen, where the sushi I ordered is waiting, but at her words, I stop in my tracks. "You did? How?"

Though I consider Natasha my best friend, I never told her about my betrothal to Alexei or our complicated, decade-long cat-and-mouse relationship. As far as she or any of our friends in Moscow knew, Alexei and I were less-than-friendly acquaintances, nothing more.

She bites her lip. "Remember that weird ring you got at my house when we were fourteen or something? You never told me what that was about, but I heard

Lyudmila talking about it on the phone later. It was from him, wasn't it? He was 'AL?'" Before I can confirm or deny, she presses on. "And the way you two were all buddy-buddy at my gala right before you disappeared on us? Yeah, that was a dead giveaway. Not to mention —" She stops.

"Not to mention what?"

She gives me a sheepish smile. "Well, there were rumors about the two of you. Ever since your eighteenth-birthday party. People said they saw him give you what looked like an engagement ring, and then you two had a fight or something. Next thing we know, your parents are telling everyone that you felt sick and had to leave early."

"I did feel sick."

"Right." She flaps her hand dismissively. "Anyway, I've suspected things for a while now. A lot of people have. And in my case"—she grimaces—"I more than suspected. I... knew."

I frown. "What?"

What does that mean, she *knew*?

Color creeps up her cheeks. "I've been wanting to tell you for a while, but Alexei sort of... forbade it. But since the two of you are married now, I figure it's all good." She grips my hands. "It is, right? You're not mad?"

"Mad about what?" I ask, even though I already have a suspicion. An ugly one.

Her grip on my hands tightens. "All I did was answer some of his questions, I swear. Harmless stuff—

like what kind of shampoo you liked, what size shoes you wore, what skincare you used. Just basic things about you. I thought it was sweet that he wanted to please you, you know?"

I pull my hands away. "You... spied on me for Alexei?"

"No!" Her color heightens. "I just answered his questions, that's all. He told me you two had a secret on-again, off-again thing going on, and it made so much sense—why you never dated anyone and never told me anything. It was because of your families, right? They were business rivals and all that?"

"You mean like Romeo and Juliet? Is that what he told you we were?"

"Kind of. You're not mad, are you?" She gives me a pleading look. "Please tell me you're not mad. I've been wanting to tell you, but Alexei said you'd be mad and not want to talk to me."

I stare at her, my mind whirling. This explains a little mystery that's been nibbling at me: how Alexei knew what brands of makeup I preferred and so on. On the yacht, I'd offhandedly wondered how he knew so much about me, whether he'd somehow snuck some cameras into my penthouse despite all the security measures or bribed some of our staff. But this—simply asking my best friend about my likes and dislikes—is something I'd never imagined he'd do.

Mostly because I couldn't imagine Natasha would answer him and not tell me.

Why would she do that?

If some guy came to me with questions about her, she'd be the first to hear about it—and I certainly wouldn't tell him anything without her okay.

Then it dawns on me, why she looks so flushed and guilty. "He paid you for this, didn't he? He didn't just ask; he gave you something for the information."

That's why she said he "forbade" her to tell me.

Because he has some kind of hold over her.

Fuck. This is Alexei we're talking about. Of course he has a hold over her.

Natasha looks like she wants to cry. "It wasn't like that. He didn't pay me anything, I swear. It's just…" She sucks in a breath. "Well, my father was trying to enter this highly exclusive investment consortium, and Alexei said he'd get him in if I answered a few questions about you. He told me the two of you had been secretly dating, and he wanted to buy you gifts you'd like, maybe surprise you with a weekend getaway. I thought it was so nice and sweet of him, you know? And look at you two now: married and happy! So it all worked out, didn't it?"

I manage to keep my voice even. "For your father too, I presume?"

She bobs her head. "It was a huge break for him. Really took his business to the next level. But that's not why I did it. I just… wanted to help bring you two together. The way Alexei talked about it, like the two of you were *fated*, like you were meant to be—it was so freaking romantic. Even your birthday is on the same day as his, right?"

I draw in a breath. "Right."

I honestly don't know how to react, what to say to her. Answering a few questions about my preferences does sound harmless, except that she was indirectly paid for it. To the tune of billions, most likely, given the dramatic improvement in her family's fortunes in recent years.

I knew her father's business had started doing better, but I didn't think anything of it. I couldn't have imagined that Alexei had had a hand in it, that he'd go as far as to bribe my friend into being his spy.

"I have to digest this," I tell her, and she winces.

"So you *are* mad?"

"I'm… ambivalent," I say, and it's the truth.

If she'd told me this a couple of months ago, I'd have regarded her actions as a stab in the back and would never have spoken to her again. Alexei was right about that. But it's different between the two of us now.

The man she sold me out to is not my enemy anymore. He's the love of my life.

Does that excuse what she did?

I don't know.

I don't think I can ever trust her again.

Then again, maybe I never fully trusted her. After all, I didn't tell her about Alexei and his decade-long pursuit of me. Why didn't I? Come to think of it, why didn't I tell anybody that he was stalking me, not even my own brothers?

Maybe they would've helped.

And maybe that's what I was afraid of.

As much as I feared and dreaded Alexei's obsessive interest in me, a part of me liked it. Reveled in it. *Wanted it.*

That tiny, twisted part of me was thrilled each time I caught a glimpse of his men watching me as I went about my life.

It was terrifying to know he was out there wanting me, waiting for me. Yet, in some perverse way, it made me feel safe. Like nothing out there could hurt me… except him.

Yeah, I'll need to dissect that during my next therapy session. Or the next dozen.

Natasha is babbling apologies now, all teary-eyed, so I take pity on her. "Why don't we have some sushi?" I say gently. "This place I ordered from makes excellent veggie rolls."

With that, we finally go to the kitchen, where we eat and talk about everything under the sun except for the full, complicated truth about my relationship with Alexei.

I don't think I'll ever tell her about that.

CHAPTER 28

ALINA

I contemplate confronting Alexei about Natasha's revelations, but I decide against it. What would be the point? Bribing my friend into revealing personal but fairly innocuous information is far from the worst thing he's done. If anything, his goal was to please me, to make me happy and comfortable—which he continues doing in so many big and small ways.

A month into our new life together in Moscow, I'm the happiest I've ever been. I'm making tremendous progress on my game, my health is improving by leaps and bounds, and it feels like Alexei and I are growing closer together... even though he still hasn't said those three little words.

I ignore it. Or try to. Instead, I focus on making *him* happy, or at least distracting him from his grief. Though he doesn't talk about it, it feels like his father's death has greatly impacted him. We haven't been together that long, but I can tell he's different these days, not fully himself—which makes sense. He's lost his remaining parent. But I can't help feeling that there's something more to it, something he's not telling me... something he doesn't want me to know.

Which sucks because we talk a lot otherwise. Over meals and during lazy mornings, in the evenings as we cuddle together in front of the TV and on the forest hikes during which we pick mushrooms—something that's turned out to be a favorite activity of his as well as mine—we talk about anything and everything, from the latest developments in the Middle East that impact our families' ventures to the best places to go spelunking, which I've learned is one of his hobbies.

I've also learned that my husband is exceptionally smart and highly knowledgeable about a variety of topics, as intellectual in his own way as my near-AI-level oldest brother. Though Alexei has never formally studied computer science, his insightful suggestions for my game have helped me get through a few thorny patches, and his ability to quickly synthesize information is second to none. I've heard him speak to everyone, from my doctors to the nuclear scientists he employs, on their level, easily sprinkling in terminology that no layman should know.

His capabilities are both impressive and scary, especially coupled with his unapologetic ruthlessness and propensity for violence.

The latter bothers me, I won't lie. Though I no

longer fear that he'll turn on me the way my father turned on my mother, I haven't forgotten all the lives he's taken in his quest to get me, and when I think about it, I feel the sharp bite of guilt and shame that I love the man who did those terrible things. Who'd probably do them all over again if he had to. But I can no longer lie to myself. I do love him. And I'm happy with him. And if that makes me a bad person... well, I am—or was—a Molotov.

Now I'm a Leonov.

———

ANOTHER MONTH PASSES. OVERNIGHT, HEAVY SNOW blankets the trees surrounding our mansion and fills the air with the crisp, clean scent of winter. The view out of my bedroom window reminds me of my time at Nikolai's mountain compound, except we're less than an hour's drive from the center of Moscow.

As my health continues to improve, Alexei and I begin to venture out into society, attending fundraisers and galas, meeting friends at restaurants, and going to the opera and ballet. All things I used to do, only now we're doing them together, and that makes a world of difference.

I no longer look over my shoulder, afraid—but subconsciously hoping—to see his tall, dark figure across the room. Instead, he's at my side, his hand clasping mine possessively or resting on my lower back. He's always touching me, always guarding me, always marking me as his. And I don't mind in the least. The rare times when he does step away from me, I feel uneasy, unsettled. Anxious in some peculiar way. When I told my therapist about it, she said Alexei has become my safety blanket because he helped me through my illness. But I don't think she's right. Not entirely, at least. My need for him is bone-deep and visceral—and it was there before my diagnosis, though I misinterpreted it at the time.

I thought the anxiety I'd been dealing with for the past decade was fear of *him* when it was something else. An unfulfilled longing, perhaps. A sense of something missing, of a pervasive wrongness in my life.

Even as I did my best to escape from him, some part of me already loved him. Craved him. Needed him.

It's as if fate had truly tied our lives together, so that one wouldn't be complete without the other.

I'm pondering that as I absentmindedly pick up my phone to check the news while I wait for Alexei to finish his morning routine in the bathroom and join me for breakfast. As I scroll through the headlines, a notification pops up—a search engine alert I set up a few weeks ago after a graphic nightmare featuring the man I killed in Geneva.

I don't have such dreams often, thankfully, but the guilt is still with me.

I don't think it'll ever fully go away.

The alert is designed to notify me of any new online

mentions of the man, Linus Bocelli—a name I wormed out of Konstantin with great effort. Once I had it, I confirmed what Alexei told me: that Bocelli had been accused of rape twice in recent years but was never prosecuted for it, likely due to his family's connections.

It made me feel better, knowing that my assailant wasn't just a drunk who'd wandered into the wrong room that night... that I'd potentially saved other women from suffering the fate that I'd almost been subjected to.

It didn't erase the memory of his blood on my hands, but it helped.

In any case, I don't know why I set up the alert. It was a whim. I wasn't actually expecting anything to pop up after Valery's crew cleaned up the scene. I think it was just a way for me to have a sense of closure, a certainty that the bodies were staying buried—literally, in this case.

Which is why the article from a small Geneva newspaper that pops up when I click on the alert is so disturbing.

The headline reads:

German Tourist Arrested in Missing Person Case

Heart pounding, I skim the article. Apparently, there's been a breakthrough in the case of Linus Bocelli, who's been listed as missing for four months. Some new evidence came to light that led the authorities to a suspect in his disappearance: a twenty-three-year-old German tourist by the name of... Birgit Schwann.

I do a double take.

No.

It can't be.

They couldn't possibly be talking about the same Birgit I know.

Frantically, I read on.

The young woman was staying at the hostel at the time of Bocelli's disappearance...

Fuck.

It is her.

There must be some kind of error here.

Why would they arrest Birgit, of all people?

Also, shouldn't she be in Thailand by now?

I've been meaning to get in touch with her, but I kept forgetting to ask Konstantin to find her number for me.

This is bad. I need to do something. Anything.

I leap to my feet just as Alexei enters the kitchen.

Whatever he reads on my face must alarm him because he closes the distance between us in three long strides.

"What's wrong?" His voice is sharp as he grips my arm. "What happened?"

"It's Birgit. Here." I hand my phone to him.

He reads the article, his expression unchanging.

Did he already know about this?

"This is... unfortunate," he says, looking up from the screen. He hands my phone back to me. "I'll let Valery know, though I'm sure his people are already on top of it."

"On top of it how?" My own tone sharpens. "Why was Birgit arrested for a crime *I* committed?"

"We'll find out," Alexei says and pulls out his own phone. His fingers fly swiftly over the screen, presumably firing off a message. Putting the phone back into his pocket, he says, "Now let's eat while we wait."

Chapter 29

Alexei

My Alinyonok is tense as I blend our morning smoothies. She's worried about the German girl. I don't care much about Birgit's fate, but I don't want Alina upset, so I will do whatever is necessary to fix this situation.

Valery's reply to my message arrives with a ding as I hand Alina her cup.

Aware of the situation. Handling it.

I reply back: *Need more details. Alina aware as well.*

I'm sure he understands what that last part means.

"What did he say?" Alina asks when I put the phone away again.

I take a gulp of my smoothie. "Nothing much yet. As soon as—"

Another ding on my phone.

I skim Valery's reply, then read it out loud:

Police found footage from the hostel's security camera. Schwann had a confrontation with Bocelli a few days prior to the incident. He came on to her in the lobby; she punched him in the face. Told him to fuck off and die. Since this took place prior to Alina's arrival at the hostel, my team didn't scrub it.

Alina drags in an audible breath. "She never told me about that. Said he was harmless, albeit a 'pervy idiot.'"

"Maybe he was harmless to *her*."

I bet the motherfucker preferred his victims weak and passive—either drunk or too sick to fight back, the latter being the category he probably figured Alina fell into. Except she surprised him.

For the umpteenth time, I wish I'd gotten there earlier so I could've sliced the bastard open myself. Slowly. With a serrated blade. Keeping him conscious the whole time as I force-fed him his own guts and—

"We have to do something to fix this." Alina paces the kitchen, smoothie in hand. "We can't let her get in trouble for what I did."

"I'm sure they'll just question her and let her go. There's no body, nor any other evidence linking her to the disappearance."

Or at least there shouldn't be. Unless Valery's team overlooked something else?

I reach for my phone again:

Is there something else we should know? Any reason this can't go away on its own?

Valery's reply takes a minute to arrive, and I read it out loud for Alina again:

Maybe. We're digging deeper into the Bocelli family in

Italy. Preliminary evidence suggests they're connected to Enzo Accardi. Linus appears to have been his third cousin.

Motherfucker. That would explain why the rape charges against him were dropped.

I lower my phone to find Alina staring up at me.

"Who the fuck is Enzo Accardi?" she demands.

"The owner of Accardi Enterprises." When she still looks blank, I add, "His organization runs Sicily."

Alina chokes on the smoothie she just took a sip of. "They're *mafia?*"

"They don't like to be called that anymore." Which I can understand.

"But that's what they are, right?" Alina sets her drink down with a thud. "The man I killed is connected to the *Italian mob?*"

"The Sicilian mob." Though now that I think about it, Accardi has his tentacles all over Italy.

Alina throws up her hands. "Why didn't this come up before?"

Good question. I text it to Valery. He replies immediately:

Relation too distant to blip on the regular background report. Were only alerted to the possibility of a connection when we hacked Bocelli's father's email this morning. A couple of weeks ago, he reached out to Accardi for help with prosecuting the only suspect, the German girl. Seems convinced she's behind it. Accardi must've pulled some strings with the Geneva police to initiate the arrest.

"So let me get this straight," Alina says after I read her the message. "The father of the man I killed is looking for someone to blame, and because of his distant mafia relative, he was able to get an innocent woman arrested on next-to-no evidence?" Then she must reach the same conclusion as I did earlier because she gasps and says, "That's how he got away with it, right? The rapes he was never prosecuted for? Accardi must've pulled some strings for the Bocellis then too."

"I suspect that's the case."

Which makes everything so much more complicated. If Bocelli truly thinks her guilty, Birgit is fucked. With Accardi's kind of pull, proof of innocence can be disregarded, or conversely, evidence of guilt manufactured. It's simple enough to do. We've done it dozens of times ourselves, as have the Molotovs.

When you have enough money and power, the legal system is your weapon, to be wielded as you see fit—which is fine when we're the ones wielding it. But in this case, it's being wielded against an innocent woman, one that my wife cares about. And, more importantly, a woman who knows my full name and thus Alina's. At this very moment, Birgit could be talking to the Geneva police, telling them all about the sick Russian woman who stayed with her—and then disappeared right when Bocelli did.

If they don't put two and two together after that, I'll be very surprised.

"We need to do something." Alina resumes pacing. "We have to get Birgit out."

That, or ensure she's not able to speak to anyone. I bet that's the solution Valery is favoring. And it's one I would choose also if not for the fact that it would cause Alina distress. Not to mention, Birgit may have already opened her mouth, and eliminating her would only bring the police—or worse, Accardi's people—to our doorstep that much sooner.

The Geneva police are not a real threat to us, but Accardi could cause trouble if he were so inclined.

Would he be inclined, though? Just how close is he to the Bocellis?

It's one thing to bribe a cop or two to indulge a distant relative, but it's another thing entirely to go up against a family as powerful as the Leonovs… and the Molotovs.

I doubt Alina's brothers will stay on the sidelines in this fight.

I'm about to text Valery with my next question when a text from him arrives with a ping:

Konstantin just accessed the cameras and arrest records at the station. Schwann hasn't said anything about Alina yet. The problem can still be contained.

"What did he say?" Alina grabs for my phone, and despite my misgivings, I show her the message.

Her face goes pale, and she clenches her jaw. "No. Absolutely not. Birgit is *not* expendable. Do you hear me? You cannot 'contain' the problem by making *her* go away. I won't have it." Her voice rises. "Alexei, please, don't let them hurt Birgit, or I swear to god, I will—"

"I won't." The promise emerges of its own accord, born not of rational thought but of an automatic, instinctual need to please her, to take away the source of her stress and worry.

Six months ago, I wouldn't have made this promise. I would've done what's best for her and for our future life together, regardless of the fallout—as I've done so many times in the past. But that was before. Before I knew what it was like to have her snuggle close to me and hear her whisper, "I love you." Before I knew—truly knew and understood—the tender, vulnerable, complicated core of her, this woman I've wanted for so long and have fought so hard for.

Six months ago, I was a man she hated—and I don't want to be one ever again.

So, even though the simple, logical thing to do would be to let Valery eliminate Birgit as he's undoubtedly planning, I frame Alina's face with my palms and tell her solemnly, "I'll stop them. We'll find another way to make the problem go away."

She inhales slowly, and I see the tension drain out of her. She believes me, trusts me, and that makes all the upcoming headache worthwhile. I lean in and kiss her forehead, inhaling her sweet scent as I do, and then I text her brothers:

Do not do anything. It's time for a meeting.

CHAPTER 30

ALINA

My brothers have visited me in our new residence before, but we've never sat together like this. Whenever they'd come over, the atmosphere would be painfully tense until Alexei made himself scarce and let me have at least pretend privacy to talk to them, to have the same circular conversations that always feel more like interrogations, with my brothers doing their best to determine if Alexei is indeed the monster I'd once imagined him to be... and whether the risk of acting to extract me from his grasp outweighs the risk of letting me continue in this marriage for now.

Today, everything is different. The air in this meeting room on the first floor of our mansion still reeks of tension and an excess of testosterone, but I'm no longer the proverbial bone in the middle, the reason the men in my life are at odds with each other.

Instead, Alexei and I are united against my brothers.

Valery's expression is coolly inscrutable, as always, but I can tell he's irritated. "What are you proposing instead?" he asks when I inform him that Birgit is not to be touched under any circumstances. "She's five minutes and one pointed question away from telling Accardi's dirty cops all about the Russian girl who stayed with her at the exact time of Bocelli's disappearance. What do you expect us to do when his goons come sniffing around for answers? Are we going to war for this German you've known for all of two days?"

"No, of course not!" The last thing I'd want is for anyone to be in danger, our guards included. "This is why we're all here, so we can figure this out."

At my side, Alexei stirs, a dark, silent presence until now. His strong, tan fingers interlace with mine atop the conference table, a possessive hold that draws Konstantin's gaze and makes his jaw tighten.

"I propose we extract Schwann from custody," Alexei says. "Right away. Before that pointed question is asked."

Konstantin tears his gaze away from Alexei's hand on mine. His jaw is still clenched, but his tone is even. "I suppose you've already set the plans in motion?"

To my shock, Alexei nods. "My men are on the way there as we speak."

I blink. How on earth…? It's been less than three hours since we found out about the situation.

Valery's eyes narrow, and then a cold smile spreads across his face. "Bravo. I suppose the purpose of this meeting was to keep us out of your men's hair?"

Alexei's smile is just as cold, even as his hand remains a warm, reassuring weight on mine. "Like you said, we get her out *now*, or she blabs. There was no time to waste on debates."

I stare at my husband, impressed despite myself. With this one maneuver, he's forestalled any and all arguments, getting my brothers to fall neatly into line. Because that's what must happen now: If they don't want this to go south, they won't stand in his way. In fact, they'll support his plan in any way they can.

Already, Konstantin's thumbs are flying across the screen of his phone, undoubtedly sending off instructions to erase all the relevant footage in the police station and whatever else is required to make sure Birgit's extraction doesn't leave any evidence that can be traced back to us.

I'm pondering why Alexei didn't tell *me* the plan when Valery's eyes flick over to Alexei's fingers interlaced with mine. "A word with my sister, please." His tone is cool and steady, even as annoyance simmers deep beneath.

Alexei rises to his feet with a sardonic gleam in his eyes. "By all means. I'll check on the progress of the operation in the meantime."

He leaves the dining room with a few long strides, giving us privacy that is as much a sham as this meeting turned out to be.

He knows, as we all do, that invisible cameras line every corner of this room, recording every word that will be said. Valery might as well talk to me in front of him.

I sigh and look at my brothers, preparing myself for another pseudo-interrogation. It doesn't matter what I say about wanting to stay with Alexei—they simply don't believe me. But they're not looking at me.

Instead, they're on their feet, already rounding the long oval table toward me.

I gasp when they grab me, one arm each, and pull me up to stand. "What are you doing?" I whisper-hiss, not wanting to alert Alexei to whatever craziness my brothers are trying.

They don't answer. Their faces are tense, eyes narrowed as they drag me toward the wall that is a window—currently not enclosed in its concrete slab so as to let us enjoy the afternoon light.

I begin to struggle, still keeping quiet. Whatever they're planning, I'm not down for this, but I don't want anyone to get hurt, as is bound to happen if Alexei realizes what's happening.

My struggles are in vain. Both Valery and Konstantin are tall, athletic men with significant fighting experience; my frantic movements barely register for them.

"Stop it," I hiss in desperation. "I don't want this!"

My brothers ignore me. When we reach the window, Konstantin slaps a tiny, cockroach-shaped metal device onto the surface. It whirrs to life, and I gape in shock as it eats through five centimeters of bulletproof glass as if it were paper.

In the meantime, Valery is attaching three more metal cockroaches, and they all move as one, cutting out a man-sized rectangle inside the window in a matter of seconds.

What the fuck are those things? And why isn't Alexei seeing this through the million cameras he's got hidden all over?

I cast a frantic look around the room, but I don't see anything out of place. Yet my brothers must've done something to prevent Alexei's guards from realizing what's happening. Maybe Konstantin hacked the cameras and is feeding them a false image? Or—

"Let's go." Valery's quiet voice is filled with urgency as he pushes on the cutout glass and makes it fall into the low shrubs outside. "We have less than a minute."

Less than a minute before what?

I want to ask, but I don't get a chance as he jumps out after the glass, landing just past the shrubs in the smooth crouch of a cat. As soon as he straightens, Konstantin picks me up and literally throws me to him, ignoring my panic-stricken attempt to grab at his shirt.

Only the fact that they're my brothers keeps me from screaming my head off as I fly through the opening and land in Valery's strong arms with a teeth-snapping jolt.

"I'm not a fucking sack of potatoes," I growl when I get my breath back.

Nobody is listening. Konstantin has already jumped after us, and the two of them grab me like the afore-mentioned potato sack and sprint for the nearby cluster of trees—just as a huge *boom* shatters the silence, and scorching-hot air blasts my face and every bit of exposed skin.

I scream instinctively, ducking to hide my face against Valery's shoulder. Then terror, raw and gut-wrenching, floods my brain with adrenaline, and I begin to fight in earnest as he carries me away from the wrecked mansion and the fire consuming it... away from Alexei, who must still be inside.

No. No, no, no! Howling like a banshee, I claw at Valery's face, the fierceness of my attack shocking him into loosening his grip on me just enough that I manage to push away and fall onto my ass. Ignoring the jolt of pain, I bounce to my feet and propel myself toward the flames. My feet crunch on melting snow and bits of burning plaster as a single thought cycles through my mind.

Alexei.

I have to find him.

I have to save him.

Arms like a steel beam wrap around my waist, bringing me to a halt mid-sprint. Shrieking, I try to turn around so I can claw at the face of my captor, but it's Konstantin who has me now and he's wise enough not to repeat Valery's mistakes. All I can do is kick backward and scream as he drags me toward the fence and the trees, away from the burning ruins of the place that has been my home for the past two months.

Away from the man I love more than life itself.

A man who may already be dead, killed because of

me… because I never managed to convince my brothers that he is what I want—that he is all I've ever wanted, even if I didn't always know it.

"Alina, stop it! You'll hurt yourself."

It's Valery's voice, tense and sharp. His words barely register through the maelstrom of terror and anguish swirling inside me. All I'm cognizant of is the desperate need to get away and run back into our fortress of a mansion that was supposed to be impenetrable to any enemy yet is burning down before my eyes. And Alexei… Oh god, if he survived the blast, he may be trapped inside, injured and burning alive.

The shriek that tears from my throat is inhuman, a sound of primal rage and torment. Calling on every bit of skill and knowledge I possess, I fight harder than I ever have in my life. I fight like the man holding me is my hated enemy instead of my favorite brother. Like he's my father trying to kill my mother all over again.

If I had a knife, I would stab Konstantin without a second thought. But I don't, so I just kick and punch, screaming and twisting, clawing and scratching, bucking and headbutting—all to no avail. Konstantin is a head taller and forty kilos heavier, pure muscle while I still haven't recovered my full strength.

Relentlessly, he drags me away, and all I can do is scream in helpless fury and anguish as I watch the fire devour the wreckage of my life.

CHAPTER 31

ALEXEI

I wait until they're by the fence before I give the signal to my guards. In a flash, we emerge from the underground tunnels into the cover of the trees and surround my wife and her brothers. The rest of the Molotov assault crew have already been neutralized, knocked out by a neurotoxic gas.

I don't know what I expected from Alina—maybe some sign of guilt or disappointment that her brothers' elaborate rescue plan failed?—but at the sight of me, she screams my name and begins fighting Konstantin's hold so hard I'm afraid she'll injure herself.

"Let her go!" I aim my M16 at Valery, who's standing a meter away from them, amber eyes narrowed. "Now," I add harshly, my finger tightening on the trigger when Konstantin doesn't obey.

"No!" Alina struggles harder. "Alexei, don't!"

She breaks free and launches herself at me. I catch

her with my free arm and cage her tightly against my side. Despite my fury at her betrayal, something inside me softens at the feel of her slender body pressed against me, at the sweet, delicate scent of her that's now as familiar to me as the way she looks first thing in the morning, all soft and sleepy, jade eyes hazy and filled with warmth as she whispers, "I love you."

Deceptive warmth, *deceptive* words, I remind myself, but it doesn't seem to matter.

Liar or not, I still want her, still crave her, still need her more than food, water, or air.

She's mine, and she'll always be mine, no matter how hard she tries to fight it.

She's shaking, I can feel it, and I don't think it's just from the cold. Her distress is unbearable to me. I gesture at my men, and they step in front of us, further separating us from her brothers, both of whom are glaring at me with unconcealed hatred.

Once I'm sure the Molotovs are no threat, I drop my weapon and pull Alina fully into my embrace, wanting to console her, even though her tears are most likely from the disappointment that her escape plan failed. Except she wraps her arms around me and squeezes so hard my ribs hurt, her face pressing against my shoulder as sobs rack her body. "I th-thought—" She's crying so hard she seems unable to get the words out. "I thought you were... dead. In the explosion. Or... or burning alive."

She's hyperventilating, and to my shock, I realize

she's melting down. Over what could've happened to *me*.

This isn't an act. Nobody is that good at acting.

Except she almost had me convinced before, almost had me trusting that she loved me, that the harmony between us for the past two months was real. I was already letting go of my doubts when my hackers alerted me to a subtle inconsistency in the camera feeds from the Geneva police station, and I realized the whole Birgit thing was a setup.

Alina's brothers—likely with her participation—invented the crisis in order to focus my attention elsewhere while they finally launched their long-awaited "rescue" operation. An operation that successfully bypassed all of my security measures except one.

The moment I learned of their deception, I activated Plan C, a failsafe protocol that no one, not even my guards, knew about.

As our cameras fed us fake images and the Molotovs' stealth robots planted explosives, my men and I disappeared deep underground while tiny gas grenades inside the fence went off, knocking out the Molotovs' support team, so when Alina's brothers arrived with their stolen prize in tow, there was no one there to assist in their getaway.

Instead, my men and I were waiting.

I hug Alina tighter, her tears soaking into my shirt above my bulletproof vest while I battle a peculiar mixture of relief, rage, bitter disappointment, and joy. She tried to leave me again, as deep down I knew she would. Tried and failed. I still have her, and now the truth is out in the open, so why am I so reluctant to accept it, the knowledge that despite everything, she still wants to run from me?

Why am I still having doubts, only now in the opposite direction?

Why am I hoping that these tears mean she regrets what she has done? That the way she struggled against Konstantin's hold and ran to me were signs she was actually glad to see me alive?

I wait until she calms a bit before gesturing to my guards to take her brothers away. Which is when I notice the tiny smirk on Valery's face and see the red dots all over my men's chests.

Fuck.

I look up.

Hovering silently over us, some ten meters above, are drones. The kind of drones I've never seen before, made entirely of a reflective silvery material that would make them all but impossible to spot from a distance.

Stealth drones. Military grade. Likely remote-piloted with AI assistance, given the precision of those laser dots.

A red dot dances over my arm.

Adrenaline fires through me, clearing my mind like nothing else can. Swiftly, I separate from Alina and back up several steps.

I can't risk the drone misfiring and hitting her instead of me.

Valery's smirk stretches into a cold, hard smile.

"You got it. Now tell your men to back away from us... if they want to live, that is."

Alina looks confused at first, but then she must see the red dot on me. A gasp escapes her lips, and she whirls around to face her brothers—and then she looks up, likely having seen more red dots on my men.

"Valery?" Her voice quavers. "What the fuck is this?"

Interesting. Is she not in on this part of the plan?

Maybe not. Her youngest brother is known for his convoluted, impenetrable plans that are often only revealed as such at the end. Though Konstantin clearly knew about the drones because he calmly adjusts his glasses, not the least bit surprised by what's happening.

"Tell your people to back the fuck up and drop their weapons," Valery repeats, his tone hardening further, and I grit my teeth but do as he says.

I don't want bloodshed. Not in front of Alina. Not when she's been doing so much better mentally and emotionally.

Even as rage burns in my veins, I tell myself that this is just a temporary setback. There's a plan D. No matter where they take her, no matter how well they try to hide her, I will get her back.

I'll uproot the whole fucking world to retrieve her if I have to.

At my command, my guards leave their visible weapons on the ground and step away, clearing the path between Alina and her brothers. I expect her to bolt toward them, but she doesn't.

As Konstantin starts toward her with long strides, she throws herself at me.

Reflexively, I catch her, my heart thudding as she wraps her arms around my waist, clinging to me with a death grip. Remembering the drone overhead, I try to separate her from me, but she doesn't let go.

"Alina." Konstantin stops a few feet away. His voice is tense. "We need to go. Now."

"No!" Still clinging to me, she turns her face toward her brothers. Her eyes are narrowed and her teeth bared, a tigress in battle mode. There's no hesitation in her voice, nothing but furious conviction as she hisses, "Take your fucking drones and your bombs, and leave! This is my home, my husband, my people"—she flings her hand out toward my guards—"and you are fucking trespassing."

Konstantin glances at Valery, clearly uncertain as to how to proceed.

Alina's youngest brother steps forward, his tone turning soothing. Like he's cajoling a small, unreasonable child. "Alina... I know this is scary, but he can't hurt you anymore. We'll ensure he doesn't come after you. You're going to be safe and—"

"I don't want to be safe!" She's all but vibrating with fury at my side. "I want *him*. I've told you that, over and over again, but you don't fucking listen! He is my husband, the man I love, the man I'm meant to be with, and you two need to accept that, once and for all!"

My heart pounds madly, each word detonating in

my brain with the force of a nuclear warhead. This is it. This is her chance to leave me—for good as far as she knows—and she's not taking it.

Because she doesn't want to leave.

This wasn't her initiative.

She... actually loves me.

That wasn't a lie or a ploy.

Valery must realize it too because he stops, all emotion leaving his face. His voice is toneless. "So you truly wish to stay? To be married to him?"

"Yes!" Alina all but spits the word at him. "Like I've told you a million times before. Yes, yes, yes! Take your drones and fucking *go*. Both of you. Now!"

Valery looks at Konstantin, and some wordless communication passes between them. Then they turn and leave, disappearing through a hole in the fence some ten meters away. The red dots disappear from my men's chests as the drones soundlessly lift higher and vanish into the blue sky.

Releasing a breath I was holding, I signal to my men, and they disperse to do damage control and salvage what remains of the burning building. Then and only then do I press the button in my pocket, informing Ruslan that plan D—the final contingency— won't be needed.

That he and his men, who were to follow Alina in case her brothers succeeded in taking her from me, can stand down as well.

Breathing shakily, Alina moves to separate from me, but I don't let her. Instead, I turn her to face me. For a beat, we just stare at each other, and then, in a single instant, we come together, our mouths fusing violently, our hands ripping at each other's clothes as we sink to the ground, heedless of the crackle of flames in the distance and the icy snow melting under our bodies.

Oblivious to anything except each other.

CHAPTER 32

ALINA

I know we need to get up and deal with the fallout of my brothers' rescue attempt, or at least get ourselves out of the cold, but after three soul-shattering orgasms, I can't move. All I can do is lie on top of Alexei, feeling his powerful chest rise and fall beneath me as I try to still the residual trembling in my body and stop reliving those terrible moments when I thought Alexei was dead, or hurt and trapped in a burning building.

Except he wasn't, I remind myself. Somehow, he was prepared for this. He knew this was coming. But how? And if he knew, why didn't he stop it?

My head feels like it weighs a ton, but I force myself to lift it so I can meet his gaze. "How?" I ask, and I know I don't need to elaborate.

He understands. It's there in the dark intensity of his eyes, in the way his jaw flexes as he says quietly, "I didn't believe you."

I stare at him, confused, then push up higher, sitting up despite how shaky I'm still feeling. "What do you mean, you didn't believe me?"

He sits up as well and picks up his shirt from the ground. "Put that on. We should go get warmed up. It's freezing out here."

My face heats as I realize that what remains of my dress is hanging halfway off my hips. Swiftly, I put on the proffered shirt, but I don't move.

I want him to answer before we go anywhere.

He shoves his hand through his hair, further disheveling his dark locks. His face is taut, his eyes black with some bleak emotion. "I didn't believe you when you said you loved me. I thought you said it to lure me into complacency so your brothers could come and take you away."

I gape at him. "What? How could you…. I mean—" I stop because I don't know what I'm saying. My thoughts spin like clothes in a dryer. He didn't believe me? All this time, as I willingly embraced him and bared my soul to him, he thought I was just playing him so my brothers could steal me away unimpeded?

I gasp as it dawns on me why he was looking at me with grim resignation when his guards put down their weapons and stepped aside, clearing the way to my brothers.

It's because he expected me to run to them.

Away from him.

He thought I was in on today's attack. That I wanted it.

Fuck.

I should be mad. Furious with him for mistrusting me all this time. But I can't be.

For a decade, I pushed him away, not caring how it made him feel. I let my fears drive us apart. I ran from him, time and time again. Why would he trust me after that? And yet... there's something more there, something he's not telling me.

Something that the dark hollow inside me recognizes in him as a mirror of itself, I realize with a jolt.

"Alexei..." My voice shakes as I reach for him. The biting cold is seeping into my body now, chilling me down to the bone. "Why didn't you believe me when I said I loved you?"

His lips press together. "Alinyonok..."

"No, listen." I grip his hand in both of mine. "You've always been able to read me. You knew I wanted you before I could even admit it to myself. All along, you've known me better than I've known myself. You would've known if I were lying. You would've felt it. So why didn't you believe me when I told you I loved you? When I finally admitted the truth to you and to myself?"

He doesn't reply, but his nostrils flare, the cords in his neck tensing as if he wants to say something but can't.

"Tell me." I bring his hand to my chest. My eyes burn because I can feel it in him, the struggle, the pain buried so deep that unearthing it feels unbearable, untenable. "Please, Alexei, is it… because of your father?"

He flinches like I've struck him with an arrow, and I know my hunch was right. There's something there, something beyond simple grief—not that grief is ever simple, especially with families like ours.

I don't push him further. He'll speak if he's ready. And if he isn't—

"She was seventeen when it happened." The words that emerge from him are filled with such raw torment that it's all I can do not to shrink back under the weight of it. But I don't. Because it's my turn to be strong for him. To support him under the weight of *his* trauma.

"We didn't know, Ruslan and I, not until we found her diary some weeks after her death," he continues, his voice like gravel scraping over glass. "But we should have known. The signs were there, in hindsight. Ksenia was always shy, choosing to hide away in her room with a book rather than go out and party. But that year, a few months before her eighteenth birthday, she started to emerge from her shell. She started wearing high heels, short dresses, the works—and for some reason, he couldn't bear it."

"Your father?" I venture cautiously, and Alexei nods, his face so dark it's terrifying to watch, like a funnel cloud about to turn into a twister.

"He came to her one night to castigate her for her choices. He couldn't deal with the fact that his daughter was growing up, turning into a woman." Alexei's face twists. "Right before he died, he called me. Tried to justify his actions that night, to tell me how sorry he was. Said he'd been sleep-deprived and on pain meds for a slipped disk in his back, that he got confused and thought she was our mother. But even if that was true, it doesn't change what he did—and what it did to her."

My stomach clenches into a tiny ball. "What did he do?" I ask softly, though I have an awful feeling that I know.

"He raped her." Alexei looks like he wants to vomit. "He pinned her down and fucked her like she was one of his hookers instead of his daughter. She wrote…" He clenches his teeth, his lower jaw working from side to side before he continues. "She wrote that she didn't fight back. That when he reached for her, she just froze. Because she was so stunned, so disbelieving. Even after it was over, she told herself that it was a bad dream, a nightmare, not real. She didn't tell anyone that it happened—just wrote about it in her diary and then hid that diary in her personal safe, where she thought no one would ever find it. And no one would have… if she hadn't died in that car crash. But she did. And now that I know, now that I've read that entry, I wonder if…" Alexei takes a deep breath and squeezes his eyes shut. When he opens them, they burn with pure torment. "If that crash was actually an accident, or if she—"

"No." I squeeze his hand tighter against my chest. "No, Alexei, don't. Don't go there. She was a *mother* by then. She had Slava. She wouldn't have—"

"You don't know that." His hand is painfully tense in

my grasp. "She was never the same after that night. She retreated into herself, became more of a recluse than ever before. Ruslan and I didn't know what happened and she wouldn't tell us, so we thought it was some teenage girl thing, and we just… let it go." He lets out a harsh laugh. "Can you believe it? We just fucking let it go."

"Oh, Alexei…" My heart bleeds at the naked agony on his face. "You couldn't have known. He'd never abused her before, right?"

"No, not like that. He tried to spank her once when she was six, but I put a stop to that."

I try to imagine it: Alexei, himself still a child, going up against his terrifying father. It must've taken a spine of steel. But he did it. Because that's the kind of man Alexei is and always has been—ruthless, determined, and fiercely protective of those he loves.

The kind of man who'd violently stalk a woman for a decade… and then go without sleep for weeks in order to nurse her through brain surgery and radiation.

I open my mouth to tell him again that he couldn't have known, that this was in no way his fault when he adds grimly, "Ruslan thinks Slava was her way of getting revenge on our father, in any case."

I blink, caught off guard. "Slava? Her son?"

Alexei nods darkly. "Ruslan thinks that's why Ksenia went to Nikolai's party and hooked up with him. Getting pregnant from a one-night stand—it was so out of character for her. She didn't date, didn't go out with anyone. And then to randomly hook up with your brother of all people? It never made sense to us."

"Nikolai did say he wore a condom that night," I say, recalling the conversation when he told us all about Slava's existence. "He swore it must've been either defective or tampered with. I didn't think about it much at the time, but…"

"But maybe she'd actually tampered with it." Alexei's lips form a tight line. "Because she wanted to get pregnant. To show my father he couldn't control her. Or to prove to herself that he hadn't damaged her beyond repair. Or… fuck, maybe because she was just lonely and depressed."

"Or maybe she just wanted sex, and my brother is a good-looking guy," I say as lightly as I can manage. "Her going to that party could've been a sign that she was healing from what happened and was ready to venture out into the world again. The condom could've just been defective, so her first outing got her knocked up."

"I suppose that's possible."

But Alexei doesn't look like he believes it, and frankly, neither do I.

What happened to Ksenia takes more than a couple of years to heal from. Maybe more than a couple of decades.

It's the kind of trauma that ripples across generations and touches everyone in the family one way or another. The kind that twists and warps your worldview, making you doubt everything and everyone.

Making you question your most basic core convictions —such as that family doesn't hurt each other. That love can't be cruel.

That those we love and who claim to love us can be trusted.

"You said your father called you before he died," I say slowly as it comes to me, piece by puzzle piece. "Was that right before we went for that walk in Geneva and met Birgit?"

He cocks his head. "Yes, actually. Why?"

Because from that moment on, he was different with me. That last conversation with his father must've brought all the pain of Ksenia's revelations to the surface, and it bled over into our relationship without either of us fully realizing it.

As my walls were coming down, his were going up.

Right when I embraced my feelings, he began to guard against his.

I don't answer his question. Not directly. Instead, I place his hand on my chest, letting him feel the beating of my heart through the thin material of his shirt. "I'm sorry," I say, holding his gaze. "Alexei, I'm so, so sorry about Ksenia and what she went through. And... what you and Ruslan went through when she died and you found her diary. And I'm even more sorry about what my family did to yours by stealing Slava. It was wrong of us to take him like that, even if Nikolai is his biolog- ical father—and I'm beyond sorry that I played a role in it."

His dark eyes widen, but I don't let him speak. Not

yet. I need to tell him everything while I have the courage to do so.

"I'm also sorry that I ran from you," I say, my voice steady despite the cold. "I was terrified of ending up like my mother... or so I told myself. But that wasn't the truth. Not the whole truth, at least. I think a part of me was always afraid that I was like *him*. My father. That I was so drawn to you because there was something dark and twisted in me, something I couldn't face or acknowledge." I drag in a breath. "And you know what? Maybe there is. I killed Bocelli, and I'm able to sleep at night. Does that make me a monster?"

"It makes you a woman who knows how to defend herself," Alexei says, his gaze boring into me. "You are nothing like your father."

"Neither are you like *your* father. Or mine."

"Are you sure about that?" His mouth twists sardonically. "Don't you consider me a monster for what I've done to you? Tying you to me when you were barely fifteen, stalking you until you had no choice but to give in and marry me? Impregnating you against your will?"

"Do you regret any of that?"

His eyes glitter darkly. "Only the last part."

Of course. What else did I expect? A personality transplant?

I open my mouth to tell him that I love him regardless when he adds grimly, "And I'd do it all over again. I'd do anything to get you... and keep you. You should know that, Alinyonok. I'm never letting you go."

He means that last bit as a warning, but I hear

something else: a promise of a future with him, one in which he'll stand by my side in good times and bad, in sickness and in health, through joy and through pain.

Through love so intense it can destroy as easily as it can heal.

I don't need the words from him, I realize. He's shown me how he feels all along. But he needs them from me. So I lay my palm over his jaw, feeling the scratchiness of his stubble, and whisper, "I love you, Alexei. And I'd do anything to keep you too."

When our lips come together again, the kiss tastes of snow and ash, of grief and absolution.

Of hope for a better tomorrow.

Alina

Two Years Later

The air smells of diamonds and expensive perfume as Alexei and I move through the glittering hotel ballroom, mingling with friends and foes alike, establishing new connections while strengthening old ones.

When we're done with obligatory rounds, we stop by the refreshment table, where we run into a pair of Japanese businessmen who want to talk my ear off about my new videogaming venture.

I wasn't expecting much when I released my game for free six months ago. I was hoping some people would enjoy it, of course, but I knew that the story was too simple, the graphics too basic to have a broad appeal.

I was wrong.

The game took off.

Immediately.

Apparently, something about it—maybe its very

simplicity—evoked nostalgia in gamers old and young alike. In posts that quickly went viral, reviewers raved about how it was simultaneously like *Sonic the Hedgehog*, *Donkey Kong*, and *Doom*, with a dash of *The Legend of Zelda*.

True, I was inspired by all of those, but I didn't think my game was anywhere near the same level.

At Alexei's urging, I made a few small upgrades and released a paid version. People bought it. Lots of people. And that's when the big guys took an interest in my one-woman venture.

Offers poured in.

With the help of Alexei and my brothers, I evaluated them all and decided to do it on my own, so I hired a small team and am developing a sequel that will be released next year on all the major platforms.

It's everything my teenage self dreamed about, and I still have to pinch myself that this is my life right now.

The only fly in the ointment—and it's more of an Asian giant hornet—is Alexei's categorical refusal to let me get pregnant. Even though my doctors have cleared me, even though each scan I've undergone has confirmed that my cancer is in remission, my husband is convinced that I'll die if we try to have a child.

The only reason he hasn't gotten a vasectomy thus far is that I threw a huge fit when I learned that he'd scheduled one. It took a major fight and lots of tears, but I convinced him to let me get a nonhormonal IUD instead.

I still have hope, though. One day, the IUD will

come out, and in the meantime, Alexei has started therapy alongside me. It's not a magic fix for either of us, but maybe one day in the intermediate future, he won't automatically think of his mother's death when I bring up wanting a child. And if not… well, he did tell me he's not averse to surrogacy or adoption.

I'm politely listening to the Japanese businessmen tell me why I should let them invest in my company when I spot Konstantin entering the ballroom. I immediately excuse myself and pull Alexei in his direction.

My husband comes reluctantly. For a couple of months after my brothers' attack on our mansion, he refused to have any contact with my family, but slowly, he's come around. The men in my life are still deeply mistrustful around each other, but my brothers have accepted the fact that I'm with Alexei of my own free will and have stopped all "rescue" attempts. Though Valery did let me know discreetly that if I ever change my mind about my husband, he has a plan to get me out. Because of course he does.

As we approach my oldest brother, I'm surprised to see a woman at his side.

More of a girl, I realize as we get closer. Slim and brown-haired, she's maybe twenty-two years old, max, though it's possible she looks younger than she is due to her petite stature and delicate facial features that combine in a strikingly cute way with her unusually thick dark eyebrows.

"Arielle, this is Alina, my sister, and Alexei, her husband," Konstantin says in English as we stop in front of them. His amber eyes glint a silent warning at us from behind his glasses—a warning that is echoed by the way he wraps his arm around her back, resting his hand possessively on her hip.

Ookay. This is unexpected, to say the least. I try to remember if I've ever seen Konstantin with a woman—or anyone—and I draw a blank. To the best of my knowledge, my oldest brother has never dated, preferring computers to people. Until this Arielle... whose gray eyes hold a peculiar wariness.

I push my confusion aside and smile widely. "It's nice to meet you, Arielle," I say in English, as presumably, that's the language Konstantin's date is most comfortable with. "Do you reside here in Moscow?"

"I'm... staying here for a while," she replies, her American accent clear. There's a fractional hesitation in her voice, a slight flicker in her eyes before she looks at Konstantin, as if for confirmation.

He gives an almost imperceptible nod.

Arielle then continues. "I'm actually from New York —well, New Jersey, if you know where that is."

"I do," I say. "I went to Columbia."

"Oh!" She brightens. "So you're practically a New Yorker."

Konstantin observes our exchange with intense focus.

What is his deal? Is he afraid I'll be mean to his girlfriend, if that's what she is? I would never, and he should know that, but to put him at ease, I smile even wider and chat her up about all things New York and

New Jersey. In the process, I find out that she's just finished college and is heading to law school, so I was right about her age.

She's way too young for Konstantin, who recently turned thirty-five, but I'm glad my brother is interested in someone... even if something about their dynamic feels a bit off.

Alexei is largely silent as we speak—he often lets me take the lead in social situations, especially those that involve my family—but he doesn't step away, not even when acquaintances try to get his attention. Even now, two years into our marriage, he's scarily obsessed with me. When we're out in public, he almost never leaves my side, which is probably for the best, as his possessiveness knows no bounds. A drunk politician who hit on me at a New Year's party disappeared suspiciously soon after the incident, and when I confronted Alexei about it, he neither admitted nor denied his involvement.

Needless to say, no man dares to so much as look at me an extra second too long these days.

I'm telling Arielle about our plans to go to Thailand next week—among other things, to visit Birgit, whose arrest in Geneva turned out to be a story made up by my brothers to facilitate my "rescue"—when Valery approaches our group. Strangely, he frowns when he sees Arielle, a rare expression of emotion for my youngest brother.

"Konstantin," Valery says, his gaze lingering on the

girl for a moment too long. "I see you brought your... visitor."

Konstantin's arm tightens around her back. "My guest."

"Of course." Valery's cool smile reveals nothing. "It's nice to see you again, Arielle."

Huh. So Valery has already met her? Why am I just finding out about her then? And why does it feel like there's something not quite right here?

Arielle inclines her head in greeting but doesn't say anything. Instead, she tells Konstantin that she has to use the bathroom, and he immediately leads her away, as usual not bothering with such social niceties as goodbyes.

I don't waste the opportunity. Grabbing Valery's sleeve, I lean in and whisper-hiss, "Who is she? What's her deal? How long has Konstantin been with her?"

Valery glances at Alexei before returning his attention to me. "It's a bit... complicated."

"In what way?" Alexei asks, draping a possessive arm around my back. His dark eyes narrow. "Anything that could blow back on us?"

I blink. I wasn't even thinking in that direction—but of course, Alexei's mind would immediately jump to that possibility, though I can't imagine what kind of danger Konstantin's date could possibly pose to us.

To my surprise, Valery doesn't laugh off the question. "Hopefully not," he says and excuses himself to go greet some business acquaintances.

I let him go reluctantly. I'll have to get him alone later, or better yet, corner Konstantin.

Unfortunately, I don't get a chance. A few minutes later, I spot Konstantin leading Arielle to the exit, his hand a constant, guiding pressure on her back.

I watch them go, a chill creeping down my spine despite the warmth of the ballroom. There's definitely something off about the way Konstantin is with Arielle. His manner with her seems almost… controlling. That tiny nod—it wasn't encouragement. It was permission.

I'm suddenly reminded of the early days of my relationship with Alexei.

But no. That can't be. Konstantin wouldn't do that to a woman. He's not a typical Molotov. Or a typical man, for that matter.

Maybe he and Arielle simply had a fight, and that's what I picked up on.

Either way, I put it out of my mind for now and resolve to talk to Valery about it later.

We stay at the party for another half hour before we head home—the mansion we rebuilt after my brothers' attack. It's now more of a fortress than ever, with a mixture of high- and low-tech security measures providing redundancies upon redundancies that would be next-to-impossible to overcome. It's also the most comfortable place I've ever lived in, with everything laid out and furnished exactly as I like it. Alexei gave me free rein in that regard, and I surprised myself by having a lot of fun setting up our home.

I even added a little nursery that adjoins our

bedroom and decorated it in gender-neutral colors, though a part of me is still convinced we're going to have a girl one day… one way or another.

Outside, the snow is falling again, white flakes shimmering like tiny stars under the streetlights as our car winds its way through the busy city streets, with Alexei's most trusted guard behind the wheel. I cuddle against Alexei in the back, enjoying the warmth of his big body as I breathe in his familiar winter-forest-and-leather scent.

He truly is my everything, this terrible, beautiful man whom I feared for so long—and now love beyond all measure.

As if hearing my thoughts, Alexei inhales deeply and brings my hand to his lips, kissing each knuckle with such tender reverence that my eyes burn and my breath catches in my chest.

"I love you, Alinyonok," he says quietly when I pull back to meet his gaze. "So fucking much."

It's not the first time he's said it—that happened a month after my brothers' misguided "rescue" attempt, in the aftermath of a particularly mind-blowing sex session— but each time, the words hit me anew. Because he knows how much love can hurt, and he's still choosing to embrace it.

To embrace me, even though I'd pushed him away for so long.

In response, I lean in, and he crushes his lips to mine. The kiss is as savage as it is tender—a brand of ownership I now welcome, a vow of a future I now crave.

It's a promise of what awaits me not just when we get home, but for the rest of our lives.

For years, his obsession was a prison I fought to escape. But as he pulls away, his dark eyes holding mine, I know I was wrong. The fortress he built around me was never a cage. It was a sanctuary.

And the monster who rules it is not my captor.

He is my guardian.

My beginning and my end.

newsletter at www.annazaires.com, and don't forget to check out this series and our other books in audio!

Now, please turn the page to read excerpts from *Twist Me* and *Dark Prince's Captive*.

EXCERPT FROM TWIST ME BY ANNA ZAIRES

Kidnapped. Taken to a private island.

I never thought this could happen to me. I never imagined one chance meeting on the eve of my eighteenth birthday could change my life so completely.

Now I belong to him. To Julian. To a man who is as ruthless as he is beautiful—a man whose touch makes me burn. A man whose tenderness I find more devastating than his cruelty.

My captor is an enigma. I don't know who he is or why he took me. There is a darkness inside him—a darkness that scares me even as it draws me in.

My name is Nora Leston, and this is my story.

———

Leah picks me up at 9 p.m.

She's dressed for clubbing—dark skinny jeans, a sparkly black tube-top, and over-the-knee high-heeled boots. Her blond hair is perfectly smooth and straight, falling down her back like a highlighted waterfall.

In contrast, I'm still wearing my sneakers. My clubbing shoes I hide in the backpack that I intend to leave in Leah's car. A thick sweater hides the sexy top I'm wearing. No makeup and my long brown hair in a ponytail.

I leave the house like that to avoid any suspicion. I tell my parents I'm going to hang out with Leah at a friend's house. My mom smiles and tells me to have fun.

Now that I'm almost eighteen, I don't have a curfew anymore. Well, I probably do, but it's not a formal one. As long as I come home before my parents start freaking out—or at least if I let them know where I am —it's all good.

Once I get into Leah's car, I begin my transformation.

Off goes the thick sweater, revealing the slinky tank-top I have on underneath. I wore a push-up bra to maximize my somewhat-undersized assets. The bra straps are cleverly designed to look cute, so I'm not embarrassed to have them show. I don't have cool boots like Leah's, but I did manage to sneak out my nicest pair of black heels. They add about four inches to my height. I need every single one of those inches, so I put on the shoes.

Next, I pull out my makeup bag and pull down the windshield visor, so I can get access to the mirror.

Familiar features stare back at me. Large brown eyes and clearly defined black eyebrows dominate my small face. Rob once told me that I look exotic, and I can kind of see that. Even though I'm only a quarter Latino, my skin always looks lightly tanned and my eyelashes are unusually long. Fake lashes, Leah calls them, but they're entirely real.

I don't have a problem with my looks, although I often wish I were taller. It's those Mexican genes of mine. My abuela was petite and so am I, even though both of my parents are of average height. I wouldn't care, except Jake likes tall girls. I don't think he even sees me in the hallway; I'm literally below his eye level.

Sighing, I put on lip gloss and some eye shadow. I don't go crazy with makeup because simple works best on me.

Leah cranks up the radio, and the latest pop songs fill the car. I grin and start singing along with Rihanna. Leah joins me, and now we're both belting out S&M lyrics.

Before I know it, we arrive at the club.

We walk in like we own the place. Leah gives the bouncer a big smile, and we flash our IDs. They let us through, no problem.

We've never been to this club before. It's in an older, slightly rundown part of downtown Chicago.

"How did you find this place?" I yell at Leah, shouting to be heard above the music.

"Ralph told me about it," she yells back, and I roll my eyes.

Ralph is Leah's ex-boyfriend. They broke up when he started acting weird, but they still talk for some reason. I think he's into drugs or something these days. I'm not sure, and Leah won't tell me out of some misplaced loyalty to him. He's the king of shady, and the fact that we're here on his recommendation is not super-comforting.

But whatever. Sure, the area outside is not the best, but the music is good and the crowd is a nice mix of people.

We're here to party, and that's exactly what we do for the next hour. Leah gets a couple of guys to buy us shots. We don't have more than one drink each. Leah— because she has to drive us home. And me—because I don't metabolize alcohol well. We may be young, but we're not stupid.

After the shots, we dance. The two guys who bought us drinks dance with us, but we gradually migrate away from them. They're not that cute. Leah finds a group of college-age hotties, and we sidle up to them. She strikes up a conversation with one of them, and I smile, watching her in action. She's good at this flirting business.

In the meantime, my bladder tells me I need to visit the ladies' room. So I leave them and go.

On my way back, I ask the bartender for a glass of water. I am thirsty after all the dancing.

He gives it to me, and I greedily gulp it down. When I'm done, I put down the glass and look up.

Straight into a pair of piercing blue eyes.

He's sitting on the other side of the bar, about ten feet away. And he's staring at me.

I stare back. I can't help it. He's probably the most handsome man I've ever seen.

His hair is dark and curls slightly. His face is hard and masculine, each feature perfectly symmetrical. Straight dark eyebrows over those strikingly pale eyes. A mouth that could belong to a fallen angel.

I suddenly feel warm as I imagine that mouth touching my skin, my lips. If I were prone to blushing, I would've been beet-red.

He gets up and walks toward me, still holding me with his gaze. He walks leisurely. Calmly. He's completely sure of himself. And why not? He's gorgeous, and he knows it.

As he approaches, I realize that he's a large man. Tall and well built. I don't know how old he is, but I'm guessing he's closer to thirty than twenty. A man, not a boy.

He stands next to me, and I have to remember to breathe.

"What's your name?" he asks softly. His voice somehow carries above the music, its deeper notes audible even in this noisy environment.

"Nora," I say quietly, looking up at him. I am absolutely mesmerized, and I'm pretty sure he knows it.

He smiles. His sensuous lips part, revealing even white teeth. "Nora. I like that."

He doesn't introduce himself, so I gather my courage and ask, "What's your name?"

"You can call me Julian," he says, and I watch his lips moving. I've never been so fascinated by a man's mouth before.

"How old are you, Nora?" he asks next.

I blink. "Twenty-one."

His expression darkens. "Don't lie to me."

"Almost eighteen," I admit reluctantly. I hope he doesn't tell the bartender and get me kicked out of here.

He nods, like I confirmed his suspicions. And then he raises his hand and touches my face. Lightly, gently. His thumb rubs against my lower lip, as though he's curious about its texture.

I'm so shocked that I just stand there. Nobody has ever done that before, touched me so casually, so possessively. I feel hot and cold at the same time, and a tendril of fear snakes down my spine. There is no hesitation in his actions. No asking for permission, no pausing to see if I would let him touch me.

He just touches me. Like he has the right to do so. Like I belong to him.

I draw in a shaky breath and back away. "I have to go," I whisper, and he nods again, watching me with an inscrutable expression on his beautiful face.

I know he's letting me go, and I feel pathetically grateful—because something deep inside me senses that he could've easily gone further, that he doesn't play by the normal rules.

That he's probably the most dangerous creature I've ever met.

I turn and make my way through the crowd. My hands are trembling, and my heart is pounding in my throat.

I need to leave, so I grab Leah and make her drive me home.

As we're walking out of the club, I look back and I see him again. He's still staring at me.

There is a dark promise in his gaze—something that makes me shiver.

————

Order your copy of *Twist Me* today at
www.annazaires.com!

Excerpt from Dark Prince's Captive by Anna Zaires and Charmaine Pauls

One minute, I'm in a hospital, about to kick the bucket, and the next, I'm in a weird jungle teeming with ridiculously oversized bugs and demon-like lizard people determined to enslave me. Nope, I didn't die. And no, sadly, it's not a hallucination.

I'm pretty sure it's going to end badly, but then a darkly gorgeous, terrifying man steps through a portal and dissolves the lizard dudes where they stand before carrying me away.

Apparently, he's a prince with scary superpowers… and I'm his fated mate.

———

This is it, I realize dimly. This is how I die—not in a comfy hospice with my parents grieving in the corner.

Not even in the operating room during some experimental procedure. Oh, no, fate would never be that kind to me.

My death will come at the clawed hands and snake-tongue dicks of inhuman rapists on a distant planet.

Shark mouths parted, they reach for me—and I let out one last, hopeless scream.

And then... *they* begin to scream.

They scream like they're being torn apart.

No, not torn apart.

Dissolved.

Stunned, I watch as my lizard captors literally melt down, turning into goo starting from their scaly feet on up until only their terrified faces are left—and then those dissolve as well.

A second later, the goo absorbs into the sand, and it's like they never existed.

Horrified, I look up, squinting against the bright sunlight and the gritty wind, and in the air, right by the water's edge, I see a circle of purple lights.

Silhouetted against it is a man.

A human man.

Or... maybe more than human.

The fine hairs on my arms stand on end.

Even from a distance, I feel his power.

It's a dark hum in the air, a visceral vibration that warns of danger.

It's like standing next to a high-voltage wire, only with nothing to shield you from the lethal current inside.

He moves, coming toward me, and my breath stills in my lungs as I make out more details about him.

Tall and regal, he's wearing a long-sleeved silver tunic over a pair of slim-fitting black pants tucked into black knee-high boots. His dark hair flows in shiny waves below his broad shoulders, and his skin is a golden shade of bronze that seems to glow in the sunlight. And his face... I swallow the blood and saliva pooling in my mouth as he stops in front of me.

I've never seen a face so starkly masculine—or so fiercely beautiful.

His features are a study in symmetry, all sharp angles and sloping planes. His high, broad forehead sits atop prominent dark eyebrows that frame thickly lashed eyes of an unusual silver-gray hue. His nose is boldly aquiline, and his high, wide cheekbones are sharply defined, as is his square jaw. Only his mouth, full and sensual, holds a hint of softness... and more than a hint of ruthlessness.

This being holds immense power and isn't afraid to wield it.

I don't know how I know that, but I'm convinced of it.

His silver eyes narrow as his gaze travels over me, and I flush, suddenly painfully aware of how pathetic I must look, kneeling in the sand all bloody and grimy. And naked.

Crap, I totally blanked on the fact that I'm naked.

Before I can do more than move my arm to cover my breasts—not that there's much there to cover—he bends down and unceremoniously scoops me up, lifting me against his chest with insulting ease. I mean, I know all the chemo during my childhood impacted my growth, leaving me smaller than average, but he could've still grunted or something to acknowledge that I'm an adult woman, not a child.

Also, the touch of his strong hands on my bare skin makes me warm in all sorts of embarrassing places. Warm and uncomfortably wet.

Ugh. What is wrong with me? What kind of bizarre trauma response is this? A minute ago, I was almost raped, and here I am, fighting the urge to squirm and rub myself against my rescuer like a cat in heat. A rescuer who's most likely not even human. That sensation of being next to a high-voltage wire is even stronger now that he's holding me. The hum of his power envelops me, cocooning me in the invisible field of vibrations that feels both like a shield and a cage, same as his embrace.

I don't understand it, any of it, but it freaks me out even more than my uncontrollable physical reaction to him.

Also, speaking of things that freak me out, he's carrying me toward the circle of purple lights.

"Are you taking me back to Earth?" I ask, my heart leaping in sudden hope.

Because that would be great. I'd even trade my newly healed—though now pretty battered—body for a chance to spend a few more weeks on Earth and see my parents… whom I badly miss, I realize with a jolt.

In general, I'm suddenly so homesick I could cry.

At my words, the being meets my gaze and says something in a language I've never heard, one that makes me think of underground rivers and dark alien forests. His voice is deep, his tone soothing, but there's an edge to it, like he's suppressing some strong emotion.

Is he angry at me?

Hoping that's not the case, I try again. "Earth?" I wave toward the portal we're quickly approaching. "Please... can you just send me home?"

He ignores my query this time, his attention trained elsewhere. I follow his gaze to the barge on which the humans are now milling about, clearly unsure what to do with the lizard dudes liquified and all.

"Hey!" I yell at them. "Do any of you speak English?"

A blond woman who looks to be in her thirties yells back in a British accent, "Who are you? How do you know one of *them?*" Her gaze jumps to my rescuer's face for a millisecond before she blanches and looks away.

Okay, so he's one of "them," not us. Not that I thought otherwise. Despite his humanoid appearance, there's something distinctly alien about the man holding me in his arms. Something aside from the power radiating from him like the UV rays from the sun. Also, judging by the blond woman's demeanor, "they" are scary—not a surprise either, given the whole melting of lizard dudes into goo.

"I'm Elsie from Cleveland," I shout back at her. "And I don't know any of—

The deep voice of my rescuer drowns out the rest of my words. This time, his tone is unmistakably sharp as he stops before the portal, facing the barge. All the humans freeze, staring at him, and he repeats whatever he's just said, his voice even harsher.

The blonde, who seems to be the bravest of the bunch, bobs her head, even as she shrinks back under his glare.

He seems to be satisfied with that.

Glancing down at me, he says something in a softer tone, and before I can blink, he walks into the portal, holding me clasped against his chest like some kind of prize.

———————

Order your copy of *Dark Prince's Captive* today at
<u>www.annazaires.com</u>!

About the Author

Anna Zaires is a *New York Times, USA Today,* and #1 international bestselling author of sci-fi romance and contemporary dark erotic romance. She fell in love with books at the age of five, when her grandmother taught her to read. Since then, she has always lived partially in a fantasy world where the only limits were those of her imagination. Currently residing in Florida, Anna is happily married to Dima Zales (a science fiction and fantasy author) and closely collaborates with him on all their works.

To learn more, please visit www.annazaires.com.